COLD SHADOWS

SHAHSANEM MURRAY

*Peace is possible if one manages to
balance the human mind.*

HERTFORDSHIRE PRESS

Published in United Kingdom
Hertfordshire Press Ltd © 2016

9 Cherry Bank, Chapel Street
Hemel Hempstead, Herts.
HP2 5DE, United Kingdom

e-mail: publisher@hertfordshirepress.com
www.hertfordshirepress.com

COLD SHADOWS
Shahsanem Murray © English detective fiction

Editor Laura Hamilton
Illustrator Varvara Perekrest
Typeset Allwell Solutions
Project manager Aleksandra Vlasova

British Library Catalogue in Publication Data
A catalogue record for this book is available from the British Library
Library of Congress in Publication Data
A catalogue record for this book has been requested

ISBN: 978-1-910886-27-4

Printed by Mega Printing in Turkey

Cold Shadows

Shahsanem Murray's accomplished second novel is filled with an intriguing and interwoven collection of events and characters which journeys through Scotland, Kyrgyzstan, Russia and Munich. Both the plot and the characters are well rounded and emotionally complex, driven by a heavy mix of violence, jealousy, greed, despair, vanity, pathos, passion and love. Interspersed with historical references to the Cold War, 'Cold Shadows' delves deep beyond the realms of a typical spy thriller, providing a powerful insight into the devastating and shocking impact on those who struggled to survive its aftermath.

Murray may be a contemporary writer, living in Scotland, but her literary style and in particular, the presence of romantic ballads, remains rooted in the genre of Central Asian literature, imbuing this novel with a unique charm and characters which will haunt the reader long after the book has been returned to the shelf...

Laura Hamilton, editor

July 2016

"Cold Shadows" is a wonderful story filled with intrigue from the very start. This book took me by storm with its gripping and surprising narratives that run right through to the last sentence.

The plot has been built around people's lives, interwoven across generations, with enigmatic and interesting outcomes.

Author Shahsanem Murray leads her readers through secret labyrinths towards hidden subplots. There is a suggestion that every thread of the story is pulled to its limit within its allocated timeframe.

I would like to say a big thank you to the author for giving me the opportunity to be the first reader. Working with this book made me feel as if I too, were part of an interesting subplot.

—Takhmina Sartova, Russian editor

It was a great pleasure for me to work on Shahsanem's brand new book, "Cold Shadows". I must say that this novel is very special one, since its unpredictable plot keeps a reader riveted until the final page.

All of the characters, both minor and major, are thoroughly developed and the same applies to the language and storylines. I would especially appraise the way in which Shahsanem has covered different epochs.

I would recommend this book without reservation, to lovers of contemporary literature.

—Marco Ibragim(F.I), English translator

Contents

Preface

This is a story which revolves around a group of disparate characters living seemingly unconnected lives towards the end of the 1980's in Scotland, Kyrgyzstan, Russia and Germany.

The 'Cold War' draws to a close, bringing monumental changes in world politics which inevitably impact on their personal lives, shattering the framework of their existence, and as the very society in which they live and work collapses around them, each is forced to adjust and evaluate their former roles, leading to despair, confusion, violence, deadly unfinished business and divided loyalties.

Robbed of their sense of self-worth, many diminish into 'cold shadows'.

'Cold Shadows' brings together a series of overlapping events, hinging on the fraught and rivalrous relationship between former spies Fred Rodgers and Schultz. Both are plagued by memories of a failed mission and unrequited love for the same woman; leading one to an attempted suicide and the other, on a dangerous quest for revenge. By default, a young couple from Munich become involved with Rodgers; an encounter which will ultimately endanger their lives since those on whom Schultz seeks brutal revenge, are all tenuously associated with Tamara, the young woman's mother...

As a consequence of a strange incident on the Moscow to Frunze train, the characters find their lives, loves and murky professions entwined, and as the plot unfolds, each is forced to battle a series of complex challenges and hardships.

The key protagonists find themselves entangled in a web of international intrigue and espionage, littered with secrets and double agents, but at the heart of all ensuing and almighty conflicts, is love.

* * *

I would like to say a big thank you to my team for their unfailing support: Sartova Takhmina, Russian editor; Marco Ibragim F.I., English translator; Laura Hamilton, English editor; Marat Akhmedjanov, publisher, Varvara Perekrest, illustrator; Alexandra Vlasova, graphic designer; and my anonymous scientific researcher who generously shared details of the career to which she dedicated her life.

Thanks are also due to my father, Sartov Abakir; my mother, Sartova Salia and my husband, Gordon Murray for inspiring me to write this, my second book.

I am especially indebted to my amazing tutor, Rolland Man, who encouraged me to complete this project, and to my literary colleague Galina Dolgaia from Tashkent, Uzbekistan who suggested turning my short story into a novel; and to S.V. Bagotsky author of the magazine article 'Science and Life in the 21st Century'.

I dedicate this book to my wonderful family: My sisters, Takhmina, Janymmyrza and my brother, Malik; nephews, Dastan and Daniar; nieces, Ayganish, Dariga and Jamal; my mother-in-law, Morag Murray; my brother-in-law, Jens; and cousin, Aygerim.

Shahsanem Murray
April 2016.

Introduction by Tychy

There is a lot more to Edinburgh than nationalism. The city remained unmoved during the last national revival in 2014, with more than sixty percent of voters turning out in the end for the UK. Nationalism is also only half of the story in Shahsanem Murray's 'Cold Shadows'. Mrs Murray is a Kyrgyz author who is based in Edinburgh, and you might at first expect her second novel to adhere to the standard multicultural template, in dutifully showcasing the Kyrgyz nation and identity. It does and it doesn't – Western readers will find the competing affinities within this book to be unexpected, perhaps even unfashionably so, and yet at the same time strangely inspiring. This is a story which will require a little unwrapping.

The book is full of fun and love. Espionage fiction normally comes in the colour grey, the gloomy tones and stern realities which are characteristic of John le Carré's international crisscrossings. 'Cold Shadows' has the classic international itinerary and there is plenty of crisscrossing but, despite the title, there is no greyness here. It is all cheerfully colourful. There are ardent lovers and happy endings and also a nice instinct for innocent slapstick. One spy's kilt malfunctions in front of the local gentry at a Burns supper; another spy, after tearing his hair out in a frenzy on a clifftop, dives into the sea to "chill down and reorder his thoughts." Hundreds of jellyfish soon put him to rights. This can be definitely placed on Roger Moore's end of the spy's spectrum.

So this isn't realism, at least as I have experienced it, and the story instead has a sing-song fairytale dynamic. Its intervals of verse might carry you back to the Silk Road dreams of the 'One Thousand and One Nights'. But where 'Cold Shadows' becomes sincere is in its qualified idealism about the Soviet Union. The USSR is, in this narrative, just like a "cold shadow," which still slants in all of its icy seriousness across history and over Kyrgyzstan. Mrs Murray accepts the USSR warts and all – there are no illusions about its inadequacies. This, however, gives authority to her book's ultimate insistence: that in the old days, people had reason to be passionate, that scientists were visionaries, and that nationalism and identity politics were always put second to the common good.

Many countries will today envy Kyrgyzstan: it is a majority Muslim nation with a parliamentary democracy, substantial mineral resources, and, even after the post-Soviet upheavals, a luxurious mix of cultures. Still, 'Cold Shadows' reminds us that the Soviets had a grander, more ambitious vision for the country.

Lake Issyk-Kul, the setting for some of this story, is famous for the drowned city, dating to 2500BC, which was found in pieces on its bed. Progress clearly went only so far for these people as well. We will be doubtlessly impressed that Mrs Murray's Kyrgyz character Tamara could have become a leading scientist and a single mother in the 1980s with so little aggravation. A UK equivalent would have never had it this easy. Yet when the Soviet Union and its scientific institutions finally withdrew from Kyrgyzstan, many women in Tamara's circumstances really went back from being scientists to housewives. Metropolitans really had no option but to become farmers again. We glimpse this feeling of wistful exile in Tamara's story, and it comes with its own separate, local shadow:

"The short and passionate romance with Bolot gave her a reason to live and to believe in something beautiful. And then bravely walk through life." Something of the same emotion is communicated through the agonies of the shambolic spies, in their pining for Lauren. Tamara may be the beauty and Schultz the beast, but they are on the same side in the cold wars of unrequited love.

Has lovelornness ever been likened before to the disintegration of the Soviet bloc? I am not sure that this is actually happening here - Mrs Murray's obvious affection for Kyrgyzstan means that she is not about to gainsay self-determination. She nonetheless retains a sharp nostalgia for the science, the solidarity, the sheer moral force, of the Soviet Union. This is not a tribute to any left-wing ism, but more to the practical pursuit of human progress on a large scale.

Readers in the UK might be taken by surprise by this. They might also be interested in the implicit, but quite authentic, comparison between Kyrgyzstan's bumps after 1991 and the forbidding terrain of Scottish nationalism. Whenever you meet immigrants from the former Soviet Union in the UK they typically hold the USSR in libertarian scorn. How curious to find woven into this amusing romance, beneath the vivid Kyrgyz fibres, the ghostly ring of real Soviet steel. And how fitting that Scotland, which has appealed to people from around the world with its openness, rather than with petty nationalism, should number amongst the settings for this story.

Chapter 1

Foggy Hill, Scotland, July 2014

"Hey! You! Filthy beast! Stay still so I can smack you!"

The old man, sitting alone in a hospital ward on a muggy July night, grew increasingly agitated by the pesky fly's continuous buzzing around his ears and tried in vain to swat it with his newspaper.

Outside the open window, the air grew cooler as an almost imperceptible breeze rustled gently through the leaves on the trees and fluttered against the curtains.

The patient was a local resident who had been brought in by ambulance after he had tried to drown himself in a pond close to the town's Foggy Hill area. After a long sleep, he now found himself sitting in a single ward softly illuminated by a desk lamp. He sat in silence, poised to smack the wily fly that had been disturbing him for almost an hour; but it proved too fast for him.

Both the fly and the heart monitor, with its jagged lines of green light, depressed him not least because his futile efforts to kill the fly were matched by his unsuccessful attempts to disengage from his chest, the tight rubber suctions which via wire tentacles , connected him to the machine.

As he looked at the streetlamp shining outside his window, he imagined that he saw in his peripheral vision, the shadows of animals of some sort, roaming the ward. These visions flooded his mind, blurring the lines between the real world and his hallucinations.

From time to time, the patient thought he was experiencing déjà vu as memories from his past flitted through his mind. To which world did this seemingly familiar lamp on the bedside table and the huge furry fly belong? Fortunately, because the images surrounding him did not resonate with any past events, he felt confident that they were part of the present rather than a dream.

Nevertheless, he still felt confused. He shook his head again, angrily squeezing the newspaper covered with pictures of the First Scottish Prime Minister, Alex Salmond and cartoons about his referendum. This was an issue, which had long divided the Scottish people into those who favoured 'Independence' and those who wanted to continue being part of Great Britain.

Pictures of politicians and coverage of their opinions on an independent Scotland, often scathing and sometimes humorous, appeared on almost every page of the newspaper. Scotland was deciding its own fate. Residents of this little town, whose opinions were largely ignored and whose quests for critical information remained unanswered, felt frustrated and anxious about their future. The Scots are not a delicate race and are quick to voice their views, often aggressively. As a result, there were many vicious quarrels between the two sides across every sector of the community. The elderly folk felt that their opinions were not taken seriously, and pubs became rowdy with loud, drunken debates.

These were uneasy and unsettled times, fuelled by an ideological propaganda, which ultimately failed to attain its goal.

* * *

Suddenly there was a creaking sound as someone opened the heavy entrance door to the ward and in the half-darkness of the long corridor; a shadowy figure emerged like a ghost, floating slowly towards the old man's room. Alarmed by the vision glimpsed through the gap in his door, the patient's heart began to race and his temples throbbed. Feeling completely powerless, he sat paralyzed with fear.

The patient's name was Fred Rodgers.

He remained seated and was breathing hard as he once more peered into the corridor. He badly needed to see the face of the person whose physique reminded him of someone from the past, but having been afflicted by persecution mania for many years, he was still unsure whether this figure was real or a figment of his imagination.

At that very moment, the medical worker who had been the cause of such alarm knocked on the door of Rodgers' room and with a flick of a switch, the room was filled with a blinding light. He removed his surgical mask and glared at Rodgers with a monstrous grin on his face.

Rodgers regarded the man with horror and as his heartbeat accelerated, the monitor to which he had been wired up that afternoon, testified his frenzied state. Hardly daring to breathe, the patient then watched the medic push a chair into the middle of the room and was even more shocked to see him pull a well- known brand of cigarettes from his pocket. The medic then sat down, in no apparent hurry, lit a cigarette, and began to blow heavy, grey smoke rings into the air.

The old man knew this man but could not remember his name or how they were associated.

Suddenly, as if in a lightening flash, it all came back to him and when the man began to speak in a familiar code, Rodgers froze.

"The blossom of the nut tree looks awesome on this moonlit night does it not?" Pronounced the medical worker, coldly.

As Rodgers continued to sit motionless, his subconscious mind rapidly processed the message and he found himself automatically giving the required response:

"The blossom of the nut tree is indeed, awesome in the full moon."

As soon as he had uttered these words, Rodgers became fully aware of the gravity of the situation and realized that any screams for help, would be useless.

He knew this man! It took only a single glance at the bogus medical worker for him to recognize the face of the murderer and the glint in his cold eyes spoke only of one thing: revenge!

"Where is she?" Shultz asked coldly.

Schultz was a former colleague, who long ago, was supposed to have collected documents from Rodgers that had been stolen from the East German Stassi. Had the operation in Budapest been completed, it would probably have resulted in worldwide chaos, as one side would have had enough information to gain a significant advantage over the other. The rivals within the Cold War had long since passed the point of just planning tactical games. By then the ideological war had crossed a line, posing a real threat of another military war that promised to be far more cruel and brutal, and this information could well have proved enough for 'buttons' to be pushed.

Fortunately and despite their concerted efforts, plans to create a world in which people lived in permanent fear, collapsed like a sandcastle.

So why had Schultz suddenly turned up? What could he want? The Iron Curtain had been destroyed and there was no reason for the continuation of waging intrigues.

Rodgers felt bewildered and swallowing hard, hesitantly asked: "Who are you talking about?"

"My wife: Lauren" hissed Shultz through clenched teeth.

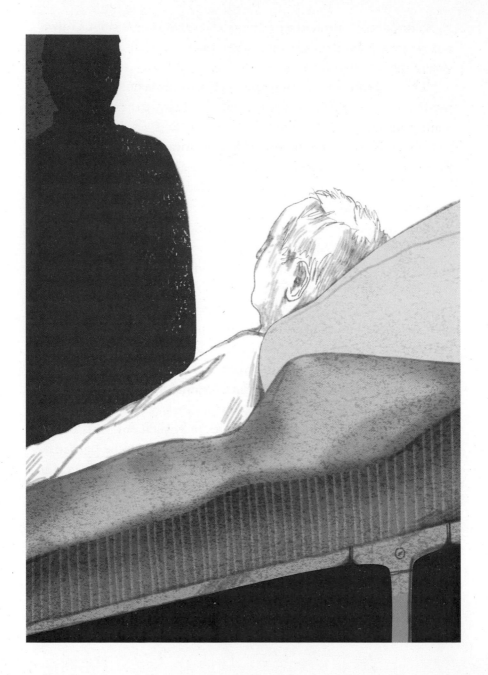

"What wife?" Rodgers understood exactly to whom Schultz was referring but cannily decided to feign ignorance.

Almost mechanically, he scrolled through a series of events in his mind's eye, whilst covering his face with his small palms.

"Don't you dare hide your face: I am talking to you!" shouted Schultz angrily.

"Oh, I do beg your pardon. Do you mean the woman, who from time to time delivered missions for us and always disappeared before I'd had a chance to prepare a coffee for her?" Rodgers began to see things more clearly and now that his fear had abated, breathed more easily. He realized that this conversation with Schultz would be long and tortuous but was anxious to hear more about the woman with whom he himself had been in love.

"Yes! The one you were always trying to pick up with your shoddy French, distracting her from her job." Shultz exhaled a final series of smoke rings, replaced his packet of Chesterfield in his breast pocket and then pulled his chair closer to Rodgers.

As the two men stared at each other, they understood just how little remained of that period in their younger lives when they had worked together.

Memories of past events transported them both far away. There were many unanswered questions and the time had come to put everything in order. Like two cobras, they stared fixedly at each other with narrowed eyes, ready to face the challenge of unravelling truths, which had remained hidden for many years.

* * *

Rodgers deducted that these were probably going to be the last minutes of his life and one by one, his memory lined up people who had played key roles in his past.

Is it ever possible to permanently shake off one's past? "No!" concluded Rodgers to himself "That is quite impossible!" He had spent most of his later years, determinedly looking to the future and prohibiting his memories from dredging up events from the past. However, it still felt as though all his desires had been frozen between the past and present and because of this, regardless of his best efforts, he knew that the memories that tortured him daily would eventually kill him. They were an integral part of his make-up and as long as he was alive, there would be no escaping them.

Now, poised on the precipice of his life, he found his mind bombarded with images of people and places that had haunted him for years, forcing him to confront the very essence of everything that had caused him such torment.

Rodgers found himself transposed to a familiar room in an abandoned building. The windows are covered by rich, heavy fabric but here and there, thin shafts of sunlight penetrate small gaps and cut across the walls and floor. It is a spacious room, decorated with a large mirror with an ornate, gilt frame. The careless arrangement of the furniture detracts from its rich elegance. Taking pride of place in the centre of the room is a unique, light-grey grand piano fashioned from the wood of a rare nut tree. Its lid is open and a pleasant melody fills the air. Shadows of people appear and disappear from view, speaking in hushed tones.

A couple standing next to him attracts Rodgers attention. The woman with a 1930's hairstyle exudes elegance, from her gown and diamond jewellery to her impeccable manners and the tone of her voice. Her name is Lauren and Rodgers is spellbound. Her partner places his hand on her waist and pulls her towards him. She whispers something to him in French, which Rodgers does not understand, and still talking, they disappear upstairs.

Rodgers had revisited this scene many times and filled with desire for Lauren, found himself fantasizing about her day and night. Hours, days and months passed by and in his dreams, he watched her as she waited only for him, crying bitterly on her bed. Rodgers, her lover, would then come to her and as he caressed her knees, she would raise her sparkling eyes to his. Fired by animal desire, as fierce and dominant as a Minotaur, he would then rip off her dress and possess her body with unbridled passion. However, wait? What is this? She is looking at someone else and has wandered far away from Rodgers. Even now in his dream world, try as he might, Rodgers cannot erase the presence of this stranger. Lauren dances with him and then they leave together. In his fantasy, Rodgers tries in vain to widen the space, so that the other man cannot reach Lauren, but his attempts are always in vain and the stranger always appears at her side.

* * *

Rodgers then pictures himself hugging a large tree and weeping bitterly for the fantasy, which he knew could never be realised. Lauren would always be unattainable and his love for her, never consummated. He felt powerless and ashamed of these secret feelings which he confessed only to himself, never daring to share them with anyone.

He had however, once tried to tell his wife about his feelings for the woman in the red dress, whom he imagined was waiting for him in that vast and empty space… His wife was now in heaven but he clearly remembered her voice: "I often think about how happy we were during our early days together, when we were both so young. Do you remember that time when we blew the fluffy heads of all those dandelions into the wind? What fun we had! Against all odds and everything that life has thrown at us, we lived in hope. We survived by never dwelling on periods of discord which occur in any marriage. It would have made no sense! Don't you agree, Fred?"

His wife had died in her prime, only 55 years old and still beautiful.

Now, as he recalled the moment when he had tried to tell her that he had fallen in love with someone else, Rodgers was struck by such an intense feeling of shame that he almost sobbed aloud. It was as though she already knew, since even before he started to speak, she had interrupted him, saying: "You don't need to explain anything. I still love you. We've lived our lives and are still together, having survived worse than this!"

Despite her brave speech, she burst into tears. She had been aware that Rodgers was growing away from her and suspected that he loved another woman but didn't want to hear it! She had spent her life in fear and expectation of this happening but neither believed, nor would ever accept, that it was their fate.

* * *

How long had the two men been sitting immersed in their thoughts?

Schultz was already finishing his first cigarette and was slowly pulling out another, when Rodgers returned to reality. He now realized what Schultz needed from him and he too, was interested in discovering the identity of Lauren's unknown partner. Rodgers had retained every detail of that night and realised that until he knew who that man was, there could be no closure. What had been the significance of their conversation that he had strained to overhear?

He had been trying for years to make sense of everything he had witnessed that night and had suffered from an emotional turmoil, which still gnawed at his heart like a worm. As time passed, the tangled images held fast in some thick web within his mind, had become ever more impenetrable.

He was now an old man but as he sat in his hospital bed, that torturous event felt as vivid as the night that it had occurred and now reliving it, Rodgers was filled with such emotion that tears welled up in his eyes.

Not wishing to appear weak in front of the stony-faced Shultz, he quickly brushed them away and waited to see what would happen next. Despite their differences, they were both held hostage by circumstances which had affected their lives for many years.

* * *

Chapter 2

Foggy Hill, Scotland, the previous day

A light, salty breeze from the Atlantic brought a pleasant coolness, dispelling the intense heat of the summer's day and as night fell, a full moon rose from behind the hill like a burning orange ball. It was a perfect summer's evening. The beautiful landscape looked like a scene from a magical fairy tale. From time to time, the long and winding roads in the valley below were momentarily illuminated by the headlamps of tourists' cars passing through.

Down in the valley, the shadows of lonely ghosts repeatedly began to emerge and retreat like a tidal wave in Rodgers's mind.

Memories of cruel jibes ran through his head. "Ha! So please do tell us all, the secret of Hungarian goulash! Call yourself a spy? Take a good look at yourself!"

Now an old man, he found his mind being taunted once again as he carried a wooden ladder towards the tall oak tree. Looking around to make sure that no one was watching, he silently crept through the darkness, using a bicycle lamp to light his path.

He had thought often about this plan, especially during the most depressive period of his life.

The mocking voices which never abated were driving him mad. They kept him awake at night and if he did manage to sleep, he would invariably be woken by his own voice murmuring senseless words of retaliation. Weight had dropped off him and his clothes hung on him like on a scarecrow.

He was even scared to look in the mirror.

Rodgers could no longer continue living like this.

His decision was final and irrevocable. He would finally execute his plan and no one could stop him. Besides, no one knew about his intentions.

"I'll show you my Hungarian goulash... Damn you all! Dipsticks!"

The old man shook his sinewy fist in the direction of a small town.

He was proud of his skills that had enabled him to meticulously plan his final days.

Whilst his neighbour was busy working in her garden, Rodgers had sneaked undetected into her cellar and stolen a small wooden ladder. Now he had brought it to a place where he had once been happy.

Rodgers emerged from behind a tree where he'd leapt to avoid being seen by a passing car and once again found himself standing at the edge of a sea of ripening cornfields. The only sounds in the stillness of the night came from the gentle wind rustling through the crops, the melodic chirruping of crickets and the occasional screeches of owls on the hunt.

As he stood alone in the darkness of that cool July night, the old man expected to feel satisfied that everything was in place. Yet he didn't feel at peace. There was something about that old story, so deeply engraved in his memory, which continued to perplex him.

As a young man, new to the Intelligence Service, Rodgers had been highly ambitious. His commitment to the job had made him wary of making friends and in order to avoid distractions, which could adversely affect his career, he made minimal contact with his colleagues and spurned invitations to social events.

There was however one exception: A good-looking French woman, who regularly delivered their assignments and always made eye contact with Rodgers. He had understood that any romantic liaison in the workplace was prohibited. He also knew that it would be foolish to embark on even a short-term, sexual relationship. Even so, he was enormously attracted to her and often found himself wishing he could spend time alone with her. He began to stay behind after work, rejecting offers to join his colleagues for a beer. He was well aware that they found his distant manner and his general behaviour odd, so he knew that they would never question his reasons for remaining in the office. Once they had all left, he would quietly close the door and walk down the corridor to the anteroom. Here, alone at last, he would pull the curtains, put his favourite classical music on the turntable, and settle down to study French. This was just one of many efforts made by Rodgers to improve his chances of attracting the woman who so besotted him.

In his fantasies, he calmed his carnal lust and holding her demurely around her waist, danced her around this splendid room, all the while watching their reflection in the large, ornate mirror.

Rodgers had never before experienced such feelings of heightened desire, even towards his wife whom he loved dearly.

* * *

Rodgers first met Lisa, his future wife, in a local church where she was giving a recital of Beethoven's Moonlight Sonata. She was an accomplished and sensitive organist, and her eyes grew aflame with excitement as her rendition of the piece transcended the humdrum of everyday life. She played as if she were flying, guided by an invisible muse, and the audience in turn, felt their own emotions melting into the music.

Rodgers was overcome with a rush of emotion. It is said that music gives us wings and this pretty, young woman had given flight to the tenderness in his heart.

He spent a long time pursuing her but she seemed as elusive as an angel in a dream and neither responded to his persistent wooing nor reciprocated his feelings.

The whole town was talking about Rodgers, and his unsuccessful attempts to snare her became a source of amusement. This however, only made him more determined. She meanwhile, was enjoying the chase and liked the way that he tried to act the clown when trying to attract her attention.

Then one day she eventually agreed to go for a walk with him. As they strolled along a country lane, he gathered up an armful of fluffy dandelions and asked her to blow their heads off against the breeze. She glanced at Rodgers in amusement and though puzzled by his strange request, decided to give it a go. Almost instantaneously, a mass of white feathery seeds covered her from head to toe and she burst out laughing. When Rodgers then bent down on one knee and asked her to marry him, she was surprised but immediately agreed.

That evening Rodgers made her a promise that he would not allow his work to impinge on family life but they both knew that this could never be so. He was called away on business immediately after the wedding and was frequently absent throughout his son's childhood. His job was integral part of his life that would separate them for long periods.

* * *

Chapter 3

Operation, Budapest, 25th August 1989

There was a certain dress code in the service, nicknamed the 'uniform'. Everyone wore formal suits and white shirts and their grey checked ties were held in place by special clips issued by the organization. Every tie clip had a series of letters stamped into it and once trained in the Service code, an agent's name could be easily derived from this seemingly random set of letters and numbers. Service rules and regulations were also stringent, as befitted the recruits' specialist training and their responsibilities.

Rodgers completed obligatory courses in foreign languages required by his post: Russian and German. He often wished that he had also been made to study French! Basic training in various types of close combat along with encryption and Secret Service surveillance ensured that by the mid-eighties he was deemed ready to undertake missions. His first assignment for the British Intelligence Service, which sent him to Poland, was an outstanding success and his career thereafter, promised to become stellar. He was a natural choice for Operation Budapest. His mission in the Hungarian capital was to make contact with two other agents and collect important documents pertaining to scientific research, which then mysteriously disappeared somewhere between East Germany and the USSR.

For reasons unknown to Rodgers, the scheduled meeting never happened and he had been forced to flee. The incident proved to be a watershed in his life and the ruin of a promising career. He would remember that day for the rest of his life.

Those had been unstable times and the streets of Budapest were awash with refugees from the German Democratic Republic. Mikhail Gorbachev's implementation of his 'perestroika' in the USSR had caused considerable changes in the political arena of post-Soviet countries. The GDR's total disregard of the political situation had led to the retirement of the government and at the end of August 1989, several hundred tourists from the GDR who had holidayed in Hungary, refused to return. Instead, finding no resistance at the Hungarian border, they fled to Austria. The Iron Curtain had finally fallen and from then on, the West was open to citizens of the GDR.

Then, soon after Gorbachev's visit to the Democratic Republic of Germany, something highly unexpected occurred: On November 9 1989, the world witnessed the fall of the Berlin Wall. The long awaited reunification of East and West Germany was a historic moment, welcomed with widespread euphoria. It also triggered broad-reaching political changes further afield. However, would this be enough to end the Cold War?

* * *

A very strange combination of circumferences led to Rodgers being unable to complete his mission and took him by complete surprise. Every spy knew that counter actions by double and triple agents posed a threat to all operations and it soon became clear that this had been the case.

However the situation proved far more complex than originally feared.

Rodgers, holed up in a secret location in the city centre, hid behind the heavy curtains as he peered out of the open window. His contact was over two hours late and he had good reason to feel anxious!

Years later, he had still been given no explanation. Even as an old man, he was perplexed that he could not fathom out why, through no fault of his own, the mission had failed.

Rodgers nervously turned on the black-and-white TV set, hoping to receive information about some traffic jam or some episode that he could attribute to the late arrival of his contact. He had already smoked a full pack of Chesterfield cigarettes. The timer on the safe buzzed, indicating that it could now be unlocked. He dialled in the code and when the safe swung open, he removed a package containing the top secret documents concerning an important East German Military Project. At the time, he had no knowledge of its content and his curiosity grew as he held the package in his hands. Later on, shortly after his 60th birthday, he would find himself trying to track down the elderly engineer responsible for the compilation of these papers.

He knew that opening the package to satisfy his curiosity was against all the Service's rules regardless of whether or not contact was ever made. He put the documents back in the safe and after entering the code to set the timer for a further hour, covered the safe with a painting of the young Queen Elizabeth.

As he continued to wait, his intuition, which had never let him down, now cried "Run! Get out and save your life!" What was his espionages' antenna picking up?

Suddenly the phone rang – three short ring tones. Placing the receiver to his ear, he heard a chilling message from a familiar voice:

"You have only sixty seconds to exit the building and without any delay, leave town. A car is waiting for you in the street."

"Sixty seconds! Damn it!" Fuelled by a rush of adrenalin, Rodgers gathered what he could from around the room. He paused momentarily to look at the safe but knew the timer device prevented him, or indeed anyone else, from opening it. He sprinted out of the room and ran down the stairs. As he exited the front entrance, his trained eye sought out the escape car – they always used the same make and model - and leaping into the rear seat, yelled, "Step on it! Now!"

As the car accelerated, he and the driver heard a loud blast and all around them, shards of broken glass from the windows of neighbouring buildings, rained onto the street. The secret agents' HQ, where the liaison had been scheduled to take place, burst into flames and within minutes, sirens began wailing as fire engines and police cars raced to the scene through the streets of Budapest.

* * *

Shortly before Rodgers had been instructed to exit the building, a tall, athletic man stepped out of a car that had drawn up round the corner. Dressed in a formal suit, he looked like any other businessman and it was not obvious that he was wearing a wig and a false moustache. He checked his watch, as if every second counted, then quickly approached the fire ladder and effortlessly climbed up the exterior of the building and onto the roof directly above the room where Rodgers had been waiting.

Looking around to check that no one was watching, he opened the hatch and lowered himself onto the upper landing. Barely breathing, he then made his way silently along the corridor until he reached a dark green door. Pulling a picklock from his pocket, he cautiously entered the apartment and closing the door gently behind him, loaded his pistol and strode towards the large room at the end of the hall. The handset of an old black telephone lay growling on the floor and the British agent who had rushed from this apartment only seconds before, had left the window open.

With a satisfied smile, the man automatically closed the window, stepped into the kitchen, and turned on the gas cooker. He returned to the lounge, removed the Queens' portrait and punched several codes one after another into the safe. When the heavy metal door swung open, he carefully extracted the documents and placed them safely in the inner pocket of his jacket.

He quickly surveyed the apartment and then lifted the telephone receiver and instructed his colleague who was still on the other end; "twenty five seconds." He placed the handset back in its cradle and exited the apartment carefully closing the door to ensure that no unintended sparks came from any of the locks or hinges. He then ran for his life as the flat filled with gas. As the electro-magnetic coil within the phone sparked into life with an incoming call, he was already running out the front door, neatly escaping the explosion that would destroy the entire building.

He jumped into the car equipped with tinted windows, listening devices and a state-of-the-art radio telephone. His accomplice, who was still holding the phone receiver, gave a 'thumbs- up' to indicate that everything had gone to plan. The two then nodded to each other, taking care not to upset their disguises. One then made a further telephone call whilst the other, opened and checked the East German documents. Having reported in and satisfied that the documents were intact, they pulled off into the traffic, careful not to attract attention from the approaching police cars and fire engines.

They had however, failed to notice the presence of a sleek black car which had drawn up around the corner. Tall and distinguished and wearing dark sunglasses and a sombre formal suit, its passenger who blended in well with the other businessmen on the street, was none other than the agent who had been scheduled to meet Rodgers.

He got out of the car but was immediately stopped in his tracks by the sight of the man exiting the building.

It was not Rodgers.

Equally unexpected, was the sudden blast of the explosion and instinctively, he had crouched to the ground using the briefcase handcuffed to his wrist, to shield his face from flying glass.

The driver of his car helped him inside and not understanding what had happened, they sat low, surveying the scene around them, before the emergency services appeared. It was then that they both spotted the car with its tinted windows and strange little aerial.

In furious disbelief that his plan had been scuppered, the agent through gritted teeth, muttered "Wherever you go, whoever you are and no matter how long it takes: I'll find you!"

Little did he know that this pledge would last his lifetime.

As the car turned and began to approach them, they could see its two occupants looking straight ahead through the un-tinted front windscreen. In the fleeting moment when the two vehicles passed each other, the toiled agent had a clear view of the faces of the driver and the passenger. Both had collar length hair and moustaches and Schultz felt the image burn into his memory.

Chapter 4

Moscow Railway Station, USSR, 22nd August 1989

"Oh my God! Somebody, please help!" cried the train conductor.

"Come quickly! I'm in coach number six. Oh, God protect us! Here, Officer!"

The panic-stricken cry had been raised by a train conductor; a red-haired, plump woman in her forties, wearing bright red lipstick and the standard railway uniform. She looked visibly shaken when she opened the door of coach 6 to the police officer.

"When did you enter the carriage?" Asked the sub-lieutenant, launching into a series of routine questions. He tried to sound calm in spite of the situation. It was a far cry from what he had expected when just two months previously, he had been transferred to deal with pickpockets, fraudsters and stowaways on the Frunze-Moscow line.

"Just now: I saw her as soon as I opened the door! I went up to her but she wasn't moving!"

The conductor sweated profusely and her voice barely rose above a whisper as she tried to answer the sub-lieutenant.

It was usual practice for conductors to knock on the carriage doors of every passenger, twenty or thirty minutes before the

train's arrival at its destination, to ensure that they were awake and to remind them not to leave behind any of their belongings.

A woman aged around fifty, was lying dead on the floor of carriage number 6. The blood that had poured from the wound on her head intensified the colour of her dark red hair. Her body was in a crouched position and her eyes were wide open, making her look astonished that her life had come to such an abrupt end.

The Conductor began to talk incessantly as adrenalin pumped through her veins "She and her companion seemed suspicious from the moment they boarded the train. They were constantly looking around and urged me to hurry up and find them seats. They did not appear to be a married couple. The man seemed a bit dodgy and was much younger than she was, and the way he embraced her, made him look like some sort of gigolo! He had abrupt manners and was very nervy, and because of his strangeness, I paid more attention to him than any regular passenger. He looked like a foreigner and wore a formal suit over a snow-white shirt. His checked grey tie was held in place with an unusual clip, which looked like it came from abroad. As a woman, I notice such things."

With her hands clasped to her collar, the Conductor began to whisper: "Holy, holy, holy God, have mercy on her soul."

"Did you hear any sounds coming from their carriage? Cries for help? Fighting?"

The sub-lieutenant checked the dead women's pulse again, as if in disbelief that here in this carriage, on an otherwise uneventful journey, someone had been murdered!

"Look, officer! The woman's fist is clenched. Should we open it? Perhaps she's clutching something?"

"Well spotted!" and as the sub-lieutenant prised open her hand he spluttered, "Here's that clip you mentioned. Perhaps they had a fight and trying to defend herself, she grabbed hold of his tie?

Is that what happened: Hmm...? Or perhaps, she took his tie clip intentionally, for some other reason?"

The sub-lieutenant tried to picture the scenario. There were many possible explanations but it was his job as a detective to find a logical chain of events. Facts that could be substantiated by sound evidence.

"Maybe the murderer was in such hurry that he didn't notice the loss of his tie clip?" suggested the conductor, breathing hard.

"You're quite a Sherlock Holmes, aren't you!?" He exclaimed, and then radioed his Supervisor to outline the situation in detail.

His Supervisor was so stunned by the situation that he could offer little in the way of advice and so and the sub-lieutenant had to wind up the conversation.

"Comrade Captain, I need medics, forensics and a thorough search of the entire train. This is no ordinary murder."

"No, Comrade Captain; it is unlikely that they were married and our situation doesn't bear any of the hallmarks of a domestic dispute. The facts suggest several alternatives."

"All passengers have been detained in the railway station to be fingerprinted and anyone who saw or heard anything is being questioned in the nearby police station. Over and out."

The radio transmitter made a grating sound and fell silent.

Soon afterwards, the medics carefully laid the body on a stretcher, loaded it into an ambulance and drove it to the city morgue for the autopsy which would clarify the cause of death.

Meanwhile, a team of investigators set to work examining the compartment but everything was surprisingly clean! The situation was more than suspicious. It had been set up to look like an accident but the presence of the strange tie clip in the victim's fist and the red circles on her neck, clearly suggested that she had been attacked and had tried to defend herself. There was no trace of fingerprints anywhere in the carriage, the ashtray had been emptied and the victim's blood had been fastidiously cleaned from the window.

It would appear that the murderer was a quite a professional.

The sub-lieutenant, who had been examining the victim's belongings, discovered a passport in her handbag. On closer inspection, the victim was easily identified. Although the black and white photograph had been taken when she was younger she was instantly recognisable by her slightly slanting eyes, the downward set of her lips and her short, thick neck, which was partly covered by her long hair.

The victim's name was Komarova Lyudmila Afanasievna and her place of residence was Frunze, the Kirghiz SSR.

She was married to Komarov Stanislav Petrovich.

As he stared at the passport photograph he muttered to himself "What on earth were you thinking of, you stupid woman, looking for adventure at your age? Damn you!"

Sub-lieutenant Zverev cursed her under his breath. He had been given full responsibility for solving this strange and complex case and would need to work diligently and for long hours , but there was no doubt in his mind that this was a murder rather than a horrible accident.

His head was spinning. Given a choice, he would far prefer the softer task of hunting down petty criminals, but now a case had arisen which would necessitate intensive investigation by him and his team, into new territories and unfamiliar countries. One of the first would be Frunze in Kyrgyzstan, home to the victim and her husband, an eminent scientist. His only knowledge of this beautiful mountainous country was based on what he had seen on television and never would he have imagined that his first visit there would be to solve a complicated murder mystery.

An expert murder detective had been called to the scene of the crime to undertake a thorough inspection; a slow and laborious task which covered every square millimetre of carriage no. 6.

He was finally ready to present sub-lieutenant Zverev with his findings.

"So, my dear Zverev, look what I have here: a cigarette stub!"

He held up the stub of a Chesterfield cigarette, gripped in a pair of tweezers.

"It must have been imported since this brand isn't sold in any of the shops here."

The detective sighed with deep satisfaction and continued with his version of what might have happened:

"There was a fight. When the murderer grabbed the victim with the intention of suffocating her, she lurched away from him and hit her head against the window. As she did so, she must have grabbed his tie and held fast to the clip. She must also have knocked against the ashtray, causing its cigarette stub to fall out. In a rush to clear away all traces of the struggle, the murderer wiped down the window and repositioned the ashtray but unaware of the small gap between the built-in table and the window into which it had fallen, must have overlooked the fact that his cigarette stub was missing."

The professional criminalist looked pleased with himself as he scratched the back of his head, whilst the less experienced sub-lieutenant Zverev stood silent.

Evening had fallen and the heat of the day was waning but the air was still heavy and stuffy. Zverev took off his hat and began fanning the air around his face. The detective asked someone to fetch them cold mineral water but Zverev could think of nothing but their case.

"We have a lot to do and I'll need your assistance, sub-lieutenant. Our first stop is the city morgue for the results of the autopsy. Her body was barely cold, since the alleged murder was committed less than an hour ago. The autopsy will also reveal whether the poor woman had engaged in sexual congress immediately prior to her death.

The detective narrowed his eyes as he looked again at the stub and then at the stunned duty police officer and conductor of the Frunze-Moscow train.

Suddenly feeling overcome by the whole situation, Zverev staggered out to the street. He felt awful.

"I have to calm down" muttered the sub-lieutenant to himself. This might be routine work for the specialist detective but for him, it was nothing like the usual duties of a railway law-enforcement officer.

Zverev was now committed to travelling anywhere instructed by his superior in order to help solve this case and realised that he might even be transferred to another unit; one dedicated to the investigation of extremely dangerous crimes. He had often thought about entering another field, such as homicide, but never once imagined that it would happen because of such a crime being committed in his district or on the railway.

When he was young, he had been an avid reader of crime fiction and particular favourites of both him and his father were Sir Arthur Conan Doyle's 'Adventures of Sherlock Holmes'. His father even took to smoking a pipe in the fashion of Holmes as he sat reading the daily copy of his Pravda newspaper in their summer chalet. Now propelled unexpectedly, into the role of detective in a complex murder case, Zverev automatically recalled the processes used by Sherlock Holmes to gather and analyse evidence.

So what did they have to work on: a possible lovers' tryst, a dead body, the stub of a Chesterfield cigarette, a foreign tie clip? This was not some fictitious tale of spies and special agents. This was reality and he, Zverev, was a key player in the investigation!

Sub-lieutenant Zverev splashed water over his face and re-joined the detective, apologising for his condition. They then got into the waiting car with its GAI sticker, and siren blaring, sped off through the streets of Moscow towards the city morgue.

* * *

Chapter 5

Bishkek (formerly Frunze), Kyrgyzstan, January 2009

Tamara awoke early in the morning and as was her habit, smiled as she raised her brow.

She slipped on her plaid, winter dressing gown and crept silently into the kitchen, taking care not to wake her daughter and elderly parents who were still sleeping.

As she gazed at the snow-covered trees from the window of her second floor apartment, she noticed that the hatch had been opened to the cellar in their yard. Tamara inhaled deeply and shook her head.

The recent surge of homeless people seeking shelter was a cause of consternation for both she and her neighbours. They complained that this would never have happened in the Soviet Union but of course, since its collapse several years ago, times had changed.

Although sympathetic to their plight, the residents didn't want the homeless camping in their own backyards and grew increasingly frustrated that because they routinely crept into the warm cellars under the cover of darkness and left at dawn, they avoided being caught by the local police. As a result, coupled with the lack of any alternative accommodation, the situation was set to continue throughout the city for many years to come.

From time to time, small children emulating conscientious adults gave the vagrants food and old clothing. One particular character became well known for always carrying a single red boot with a broken heel under his arm. While many citizens found this mildly amusing, Tamara always felt deeply saddened by the realisation that even the most brilliant mind can be badly affected by such abject poverty.

The sight of the open hatch dismayed Tamara but for different reasons than those of her neighbours.

Five years previously, her general attitude to both the homeless and the circumstances in which they were forced to exist, had changed radically through one particular encounter.

It was her custom to reach into her pocket for small change whenever she passed a beggar sitting on the street but on that day, as she reached down to throw the coins into his tin, she was shocked to see the familiar face of the supervisor of the laboratory in which she had worked.

Tamara tried to talk to the broken man, repeatedly calling his name: "Stanislav Petrovich, is that you? Professor?"

When he failed to respond, Tamara began to cry. He seemed to have lost all hope, trust and the very meaning of life.

His whole appearance – his empty, downcast eyes, trembling hands, long, grey hair and broken glasses- reflected the sad reality of his current life.

After a while, he began to murmur and Tamara clearly made out the words: "Tomorrow I will defend my topic… Will you be there? Who are you?"

Tamara took him to the city hospital, where she asked doctors to take special care of her former colleague. She visited him regularly and often brought him hot, homemade meals. Tamara made it her mission to save Stanislav Petrovich. She began by looking for his wife at their old address but learnt that their building had been demolished long ago to make way for a new city block. She then asked around the neighbourhood and discovered that his wife had run away with some young man, secretly selling their house and taking the money with her. No one knew of her whereabouts. The news angered and frustrated Tamara: she could not imagine what other horrors had affected the life and career of this eminent scientist. She spent many sleepless nights trying to think of how she could help her former supervisor.

When she next visited the hospital, she was shocked to hear that after a few weeks in the ward, the professor had walked out and disappeared without trace.

Desperate to find him, she contacted other hospitals and finally discovered that he had been admitted to the city's psychiatric clinic. Here, he was well known for frequently wandering off but he always returned, full of apologies. Tamara felt relieved but when his doctor told him that she had been asking after him, the professor had begged him on bended knee, to never allow her to visit him again. She remembered the professor as a small, slightly built man with a vivacious nature. He always wore a long green coat, whatever the weather, and old, black framed spectacles with thick lenses. He had the abstract, slightly eccentric air of a gifted and dedicated academic, seemingly indifferent to his immediate surroundings and constantly peering into the far distance.

The scientist had often invited his colleagues to his home where they were treated to delicious dishes, including homemade pickles and Atlantic herring marinated in black pepper and fresh fennel. Only the highest quality wheat vodka was served, in little crystal glasses decorated with bands of gold leaf.

His wife, with her slightly hunched back, always wore the same bright red, knitted cardigan and tended to remain in the kitchen, busying herself with cooking and slicing up fresh Borodinsky bread. Generally inhospitable, she often snuck off to her room without saying goodbye to their guests. Although her behaviour made the guests feel uncomfortable, it never seemed to upset her husband, who paid little attention to her rudeness. By the time the guests left for home, it was usually late into the night.

The professor, who was their senior supervisor, was fond of making many toasts punctuated with long thoughtful pauses "So... my friends........ pretty soon I'll have completed my research.... I've spent almost all of my life working towards this moment! I hope to be invited back to Moscow to defend my thesis or even present it in the Democratic Republic of Germany..."

After such announcements, he would smile and remove his glasses but although his dark blue eyes registered his aspirations, they barely disguised an underlying, weary sadness.

It was common for him to get very drunk at parties and engage in fierce disputes with his colleagues. They in turn, accepted and excused his behaviour: they knew that it was his way of venting his frustration about being unable to implement his ideas or have them professionally acknowledged further afield.

On the mornings following these sessions, he would greet everyone coldly before retreating to his office where he would remain for the rest of the day.

This incident taught Tamara to look at everything that had happened in a different light. Out of frustration, she sometimes acted impulsively and often cried at night, but eventually, had to concede that it was simply impossible to help or save everyone.

Manifestations of life's harsh realities, following the collapse of the Soviet Union, were widespread and hit the intelligentsia particularly hard.

People had to adjust if they were to remain sane!

Many of her co-workers, who had emigrated after the closure of their laboratory, appreciated Tamara's talents and had invited her to join them on various projects. This would have provided her with a much welcomed income but Tamara could not imagine how she could ever leave the country or move so far away from her small daughter and elderly parents. Very few of her circle who were still at home, had been able to adapt to the radical changes in their workplaces and many had been forced to leave their jobs and start up small businesses to support their families.

As difficult as things were, Tamara managed to secure a teaching post in a science department of one of the city's higher education institutes and found a new peace and confidence through transferring her knowledge to young students.

Her inexhaustible energy and hope helped her survive during these harsh years but sometimes she despaired whether she would ever again find a job that would offer such fulfilment as that enjoyed in her youth. Her desire to recapture the love that had once impassioned her also seemed like an untenable dream. Time flowed quickly, slipping through her fingers, like quicksand.

Taking a deep breath, Tamara poured milk over her strong morning coffee.

* * *

Her daughter would soon be leaving for the airport. After the winter break, she was flying back to Munich, where she had lived for the past four years; first studying languages at college and then working at one of Bavaria's universities.

Tamara quietly sang Frank Sinatra's 'Strangers in the Night'. The song was one of her favourites and its magical tale of a random encounter with an invisible lover, promised single women like her, the possibility of serene love and happiness. It gave her a secret spark of hope that washed the sadness from her eyes. A picture on her apartment wall by an unknown artist complemented her romantic outlook. It depicted a young woman with long hair standing on the shore of a lake, with hillocks in the distance. Wearing a hat and firmly holding a pretty, blue umbrella, she is turning away from the world of the viewer. The painting conjured up the sound of soft rain; a gift of nature. For Tamara, the atmosphere invoked by the image, filled her with a sense of peace and well-being. The more she studied the picture, the more it seemed that the artist knew her thoughts and inner world, and had encapsulated her emotions and philosophy of life.

She failed to notice the devastating affect which the image had on her at certain moments…
The sound of the light breeze
Sang alongside the rain.
And their music gently stroked the beautiful umbrella,
Her soul merged with nature
Sharing one language
But there was something unsettling about
The thick mist which surrounded everything
With its thick, fluffy pelt.
Beneath the light waves
Everything sang in unison with the melody

Being played in her imagination.
It amused itself with a burning hope
For an end to her search for an answer
To love's illusion
Its voice could be heard in every tune.
The Earth bathes in the crystal morning dew,
Naive to the hardship of destiny.
She imagined that:
A sudden flash of lightening
Promised harmony at sunrise
On the far side of the shore,
And that Nature's magic
Would make her dreams come true.
The light breeze which tickled the waves,
Pushing them gently onto the beach,
Would carry love to the shores of her life.
She only wanted to be left alone
So she could hear the sound of the rain
But the sea whispered its own serenade
My feelings for you are hidden
In a forgotten corner of my heart,
And here they will stay until
The day when I can express my emotions
Without words
But for now, we belong to those souls,
Lost in the great universe.
Even though our wings might be broken
We are ready to fly across the
Limitless surfaces of the oceans
Forever, hopeful

Let me be your nectar
The fruit to satisfy your desire
We must lose ourselves in the moment
And cleave together
Playing out the passion
That lives in our imaginations.
You are like a ghost walking
On other side of the shore
You are a silent echo
That rings in my heart
In tune with the sound
Of the rain
You are my inspiration,
You are my peaceful night,
I long for you to visit
The dreams of my future
And there, hold me fast,
In a warm, safe embrace.
She was ready to accept all of the happiness
Gifted by to her by destiny.
She would listen to the
Whispering wind and
The songs of the rain.
She would let her imagination
Take flight on angel's wings
Away from this painted scene
With its monochrome landscape
And one day,
Cross the bridge of dreams
From illusion to reality

In his arms, they would together
Sing one sweet song beneath the rain
And find everlasting love
In this fragile world
On the other side of the shore

* * *

Tamara often switched on a very old radio, which she had found in the basement of her parents' country house. She was fond of it despite the fact that it frequently refused to work! She had carefully tried to restore it by calling upon the few technical specialists who remained in the city. Many of those with knowledge of Soviet- made equipment had long ago left for Russia. By virtue of her activities, Tamara had a good understanding of new technology but this did not mean that she dismissed the old. Instruments like the old radio had a nostalgic charm that reminded her of the happy days of her childhood.

On her birthday, her daughter had given her the latest PC so that even if they were far apart, they would still be able to communicate via Skype. It was a relief to that she no longer had to queue for access to the internet in clubs filled with young people playing all sorts of weird games. In some clubs, the number of people crammed into a small space sometimes made it impossible to get a seat and the crowded atmosphere made it difficult for her to focus on her work or talk to her beloved daughter.

She carefully turned on the old beige radio and tried to tune in, but apart from emitting an unpleasant screech, the old appliance refused to respond. The loud, grinding sound soon awoke her daughter.

"Good morning, Mum. Why didn't you wake me?"

Sleepy Ayganysh hugged and kissed Tamara and ran into bath-room with her phone in her hand.

The old radio coughed into life and Tamara turned down the volume without having caught the morning news, then suddenly sat down on a stool and began to cry.

She had every reason to feel sad.

* * *

Chapter 6

Tamara

Back in her student days, her father often visited Leningrad on party business or missions and had always called to see her. In her final academic years he had grown unwell and spent more time visiting resorts and sanatoriums. Worried about her father, Tamara had decided to return to her hometown after graduating to be closer to her family. After working in a small laboratory, she gained sufficient experience to be transferred by the State to work on one of the city's secret projects. Tamara was able to combine her studies with her job, which brought her a great deal of pleasure and satisfaction. She enjoyed her experimental research for the State laboratory and at the same time, the workshops that she conducted, gave Tamara a chance to hone her teaching skills. The place where she worked was closed to the public and it was here that she became acquainted with some of the country's most intellectual academics and eminent scientists.

* * *

Tamara first met Bolot at the summer seminar of the Academic Council, held on the shores of Lake Issyk-Kul. She and her staff were given practical training in new technology to be used in their research and were involved in testing new equipment. Work on the creation of top-secret products always began immediately after a generous breakfast. Then, remove dressed in their white coats, the Scientists would walk down the long corridor to the lakeside lab where they would remain until late afternoon.

"Well, try another option!" The diver, still wearing his wetsuit, was insistent in his discussion with the security officers. He was clearly dissatisfied about something and had forbidden all of the staff to go for lunch. His uncharacteristic overbearing and strict manner puzzled many of the project's participants.

However, the next day, following the completion of the next round of tests, the diver lifted his facemask and looking satisfied, gave a 'thumbs up' sign. With no reason to either linger or pass comment, the staff tired after a day's work, wandered off to their rooms to rest.

The sun had warmed up the lake and so Tamara and two students decided to escape during the rest hour. It was a hot day and anxious not to miss the chance to swim in the warm water, they did not stop to tell anyone where they were going.

As they dived in they couldn't hold back their expressions of glee "The water is so warm! It's as pure as fresh milk!"

The girls chatted happily as they swam and the lake seemed to welcome their presence.

The water was so clear that they could see right down to the bottom and watched with delight, as shoals of small fish swam beneath them. In the distance, the high snowy mountains presided over the landscape like huge warriors guarding this unique gem whilst closer by, little gulls flitted over the surface of the water, occasionally diving down to catch fish.

"You've swum too far out Tamara! Have you no fear?" The serious tone belonged to a stranger emerging from under the water, alarming Tamara and her friends as they swam.

"My name is Bolot, and yours is Tamara, is it not?"

The formidable looking diver spoke quickly, without waiting for an answer, as he playfully engaged with the girls.

"You scared us, Bolot! But it's very nice to meet you." Covered in goose bumps, with wet hair plastered to her head, Tamara leant on the buoyancy aid that the diver was dragging behind him. As they continued to swim slowly towards the shore, her two friends subtly moved away to allow them to speak alone.

For Bolot and Tamara these were to be their most memorable moments of an irrational and yet passionate short romance. It felt like the warm silent lake belonged only to them.

Their following meetings were frequent and filled with something special and delicate. Was it love, mere flirtation or just a fleeting romance: Or perhaps all three?

Every morning after breakfast, the whole group excitedly discussed the growing romance, but Tamara studiously paid no attention to the whispering gossips.

During that time, she often thought about Leningrad's Hermitage Museum: a priceless heritage of the Russian people and a wonderful world of elegance and arts, which she liked to visit after her lectures. Like a magnet, she found her attention drawn to one particular sculpture made of light blue stone. It made her feel as if she were swimming through a dream world. Masterfully worked, 'The Eternal Kiss', depicts young lovers caught in the throes of passion of first love and captures the imagination by inviting viewers to plunge into a world of bodily pleasure.

"Ah, what a beautiful romance... - Mm"

Now standing in her kitchen, Tamara thought again about the sculpture's sensuality and soon found her thoughts wandering further away, back to those days at Lake Issyk-Kul.

Her beloved Bolot is at her side. They are young and full of life as they walk barefoot along the beach, holding hands. They enjoy long conversations but more often, their feelings speak for themselves. And when they stop to cling to one another in a passionate embrace, all is silent apart from the harmonious beat of their two hearts.

Such memories crept up on Tamara and she now had to try to recover her senses, completely oblivious to the tears rolling down her cheeks. The short and passionate romance with Bolot, gave her a reason to live and to believe in something beautiful, and then bravely walk through life.

"But now, all of that is a thing of the past" thought Tamara regretfully.

Tamara vividly recalled her final conversation with Ayganysh's father. He had spoken to her gently but persuasively:

"Tamara, do not wait for me."

Bolot had smoked nervously, stubbed out his cigarette, and without finishing his tea, had headed for the door. He had then turned back and pulling Tamara into a tight embrace against his chest had kissed her passionately on the lips:

"Remember: I'll always be there for you."

Without a backward glance, he asked her not to follow him, and left the room.

They had not seen each other since. She lost track of time, but on each of her birthdays, she received a large bouquet of roses in a transparent box.

Only she could have an 'invisible lover'!

Tamara did not know how to reach him to tell him that he had a daughter.

When she was pregnant, she found Bolot's sister's address through a friend and tried to speak to her. When she had knocked at the door and was confronted by a grim and stony-faced woman, she realised that it was a bad idea and decided that it would be better to keep her secret to herself. Not wishing to cause any fuss, Tamara apologized for disturbing her and instead, pretended that she was looking for directions to another house. The sister's response was hostile.

"We get all sorts of people hanging around here, including those with huge bellies. Did you see a sign saying: 'Help desk'? Go away from here! Come on, go!"

It took Tamara a long time to recover from such rough treatment from the sister of the man who she loved so fervently and passionately, and whose child she was carrying.

Deeply upset and not really understanding what this woman had meant, Tamara had mumbled something and walked off aimlessly. It was already evening. She decided to walk to the bus stop and take any route in order to leave that place as quickly as possible and never return!

It was some time before she recognized a district that looked familiar. Tamara stepped off the bus, breathless and tearful. Close to her house, stood a slender maple tree and its magnificent leaves, already turning a yellowish red, predicted an early autumn. Mechanically, she hugged the beautiful maple and feeling desolate, cried long and hard. It was such a shame: the father of her child did not know about the imminent birth of his daughter and she felt truly crushed by the rude attitude of that disrespectful woman, the aunt of her unborn baby. These moments of despair, gave her a reason to think that the whole world was a cruel place.

Realizing that she would be raising her baby alone, she started to cry again.

She now had no one with whom to share her joyful news except her parents.

* * *

Tamara became fascinated by the Druid horoscope. It said that every tree and every flower is associated with human nature and held inexhaustible, magic power.

The maple tree that grew in front of her window nurtured and fuelled her with its powerful energy. At weekends, Tamara often stood for a long time under the tree and was surprised that as she leant against it, it somehow emitted a special and invisible power that made her life feel more harmonious and at one with the world.

The maple tree is thought to be an incarnation of vivacity and coquetry.

The predominant feature of individuals associated with the maple is restrained courage. They make the most risky decisions. Moreover, they pursue a special interest in life beyond material factors. They are openly friendly to other people and are naturally sincere, never judging others' mistakes or secrets. The maple always tries to stay on board, supporting extravagant plans and new ideas. However, through helping others, such people rarely implement plans to benefit themselves. They have multi-facetted characters and an eternal quest for love. They prefer for everything to be out in the open and have no time for hearsay or idle talk.

Knowledge of the Druid horoscope often impelled Tamara to believe that this tree had not been planted under her window by chance. The beautiful and strong maple fully embodied Tamara's personality and allowed her to keep her little secrets.

* * *

Tamara did not like farewells, so she booked a taxi in advance, looked at her watch and wiped away her tears. In the bathroom she quickly applied light make-up and brushed out her well-cut bob hairstyle, which unchanged since her student days, made her look somewhat flirtatious. She determinedly pushed aside any feelings of anxiety and loneliness and standing tall, with her full lips closed tight, concentrated on looking confident and self-assured. Tamara had learned long ago that there was no room in her life for self-pity or any outward sign of weakness, and she was quietly proud of her resistance to the less than easy fate of being a single mother. Every woman has a dream: to feel attractive, to find love and one day, wear her mother's veil, which waits for her amidst other precious mementos and ornaments in a special box.

Tamara had always imagined that she would find the most wonderful, handsome and caring husband. They would be the perfect duo who complemented each other completely.

In her dream world, everything unfolded like something out of an old, romantic film: They would dance the waltz together until dawn, then meet the sunrise; ready to embrace an idyllic family life. However, it all seemed but a marvellous dream, which in her world, only existed when she listened to Frank Sinatra's seductive crooning of magical love songs.

She gently sighed and shrugged her shoulders. How ridiculous! At such moments, she quietly pinched herself to return to the harsh reality of her life.

Tamara had admirers. She still had a slim waist and well-preserved figure, which attracted attention from men and gave her reason to think that she could still find true love. However, she wanted something special. Perhaps her first romance still knocked at her heart. Part of her past, the happiness that lingered, was revealed whenever memories accidently dislodged the dust and cobwebs which lay over it. She chuckled. At weekends, she occasionally watched black and white movies about fairy-tale love that took her back to her youth. She thought about how her life could have taken a different direction. If only Alexei…

Whenever Tamara thought about him, she felt her cheeks blush. "What an optimist I am!" She mused, smiling at her reflection in the mirror.

A minute later, nose powdered and eyes mirroring her fresh determination, she walked into the kitchen to cook breakfast.

* * *

Chapter 7

Young Love

Yet still, something had stirred in her memories that she could not shake off. Tamara smiled as she mentally revisited a certain event.

Professor Komarov's assistant, a postgraduate named Alexei, had led the project. He was tall and broad-shouldered with a slight curl to his hair. His dark blue eyes, set deep in his handsome face, were as fathomless as a mountain lake.

When it was time for the group to leave, he knocked on the door of Tamara's room. Alexei was very displeased, but he tried to hide his emotions and stick to the point of his visit.

"The whole group has been ready to leave for well over an hour and we've had to keep the bus waiting for you, Tamara. Are you okay?" He asked, looking straight into her eyes.

Tamara felt like she had been struck by lightning. She felt totally bewildered for a second but tried not to show her embarrassment.

"Everything is fine, Alexei. The girls and I decided to have a swim in the lake before leaving; that's why we came in so late. Who knows whether we'll be back this year?" Tamara surreptitiously looked at her team leader, while trying to hide her blushing cheeks as she delivered this ridiculous lie.

Alexei was well aware of what had really been going on but politely apologized for disturbing her and urged her to hurry onto the bus. He didn't speak another word to her as they drove towards the city.

Tamara felt confused each time she met Alexei. His look of reproach, despite his attempts to appear indifferent, made her shudder. However at that time, her meetings with Bolot were far more important. When she was with him, she felt as though she had entered a zone beyond reality, alienated from everything around them. Looking for a passion as intense as that encapsulated by the eternal embrace of the figures in the sculpture, she submitted herself completely to her emotional impulses.

Yet, Tamara tried to hide her romantic emotions from those around her. She did not want to share them with anyone except Bolot but she didn't know why.

So many years had passed, yet Tamara could not forget the shame she had felt in front of her colleague, that day.

When she gave birth to her daughter, Alexei was the first to arrive at the hospital and bearing a huge bouquet of white roses, warmly congratulated her on behalf of the team.

Later, he found countless reasons to visit her and her little Ayganysh, sometimes telling her that he needed an excuse not to go to his aunt's chalet to help tend her beloved garden!

Alexei remained attentive until he moved to Moscow after the closure of the project. Even then, he regularly called and wrote her letters. He and his parents then immigrated to Israel.

Tamara often thought fondly about Alexei - a real gentleman as well as a prominent scientist - and she missed his company.

* * *

Tamara always prayed for her daughter and was proud of her success. As they said goodbye at the door, she realized that her daughter had suddenly grown into a beautiful and mature young woman. She also noticed an unusual sparkle in her eyes...

"Oh my God!" thought Tamara "I think she's in love. Why didn't she tell me? We've never had any secrets between us! All the time she's been here, she's been on her laptop constantly - so that's who she's been whispering with at night... Hm!"

Tamara wasn't brave enough to ask her daughter outright but looked at her curiously.

Ayganysh was well aware that her mother was desperate to ask her many questions, but simply embraced her tenderly and quietly whispered in Tamara's ear:

"Mum, I beg you, don't worry! I'm an adult and yes, I have a boyfriend."

With a twinkle in her eye and a charming smile, she did not elaborate and instead, hugged and kissed Tamara:

"You need to think about yourself. Please don't come to see me off. I know that you don't like farewells." Ayganysh waved as she got into the taxi and didn't look back as it drove away.

She was in a hurry, as if her boyfriend was waiting for her round the corner.

"Well, she is her father's daughter, after all!" Tamara thought with a deep sigh. She wiped her tears and set off to work.

* * *

Music walks side by side with our consciousness.
It sings in unison and provides respite at nightfall

But sometimes we push certain feelings
Into corners or shut them out completely
So let us put aside intellect and simply surrender to our emotions
And in these fleeting moments, calm our breathing
So that nothing becomes lost in empty, worthless chaos
Treat time with respect
Allow your consciousness to slide now and then, into oblivion.
But do not promise "eternal love" even to yourself.
Let the air flow freely through your heart
And it will thank you by aiming for something higher
If you try too hard to strive for long awaited moments in your
life
The emotional fireworks will force you to play two roles;
Those of both Romeo and Juliet

* * *

Chapter 8

Foggy Hill, Scotland: July, 2014

It was a typical day in a town on the border of England and Scotland.

The strangely named Foggy Hill is unique and has its own particular atmosphere, quite different from its neighbouring towns.

Its buildings, constructed during the reign of Queen Victoria, offered an attractive array of fine architecture, much cherished by locals and admired by tourists interested in the town's history.

Next to this town are the ruins and few remaining sections of Notrom Castle. Earl Notrom constructed its first walls at the beginning of 1400 when he took over the estate and completed the castle in 1440. Over the years, Notrom attained a special place in the history of Scotland as the centre of Druid mythologies. The legendary status of the castle continues to attract much attention, enhanced by the mystical, melodic sound which the wind makes when it coasts around the ancient, dilapidated walls. At times like these, it is easy to imagine that the history of the place coexists with the present, and some tourists even fancy that they witness ghosts of soldiers feasting or preparing for one of the military operations described on the placard at the entrance gate to the castle grounds.

Here, the summer solstice is particularly significant, drawing huge crowds from far and wide. At midnight, when the full moon climbs from behind the hill, bathed in an amber glow, there is an indescribable sense of magic and onlookers are filled with delight when a milky light washes over the site, giving them a sense of being enveloped by the universe.

When illuminated by the full moon, hanging like a vast globe over its walls, the ruined castle seems to crouch like the enormous shadow of some enigmatic animal on the other side of the lawn. However, the real mystique of the ruin lies within a secret basement, from which sometimes, the sound of a faint melody can be heard. This is the castle's most treasured secret.

Locals visit the site infrequently, in contrast to the large numbers of tourists who drawn by curiosity, often stay for several days. For some reason, it is impossible for any of them to take high quality photographs of the place... Most of those gathered for the summer solstice stay up all night, eager to embrace all of nature's wonders, before retiring to their tents in the temporary campsite next to the abandoned castle. Young lovers wooed by the romance of the setting, declare their love for each other whilst other visitors find themselves emotionally overwhelmed by the spirituality of the landscape with its silvery stream and velvet hills fringed by forest. Musicians too, are interested in connecting with nature during this special time and improvise their music by playing in harmony with the sounds of the wind and water.

* * *

Chapter 9

Stefan and Ayganysh

Amongst the many visitors to Notrom Castle that summer, was a young married couple from Munich. Stefan and Ayganysh had been carefully planning this dream trip since they got married three years ago, but it had been cancelled several times. At last, they were here and were very excited to see for themselves, the legendary place about which they had read. On their way, they had stopped at local areas of natural beauty and had posted photographs and impressions to share with friends on Facebook.

They had travelled in an old vehicle made back in 1949; a green Volkswagen that had been a wedding gift from Stefan's grandpa who lived in Leipzig.

The gift of this rare, retro car more commonly found in Munich's museums, was of great significance to Stefan. His grandparents remained the heads of his family and every year they all returned to Leipzig to spend Christmas with the elderly couple. It was always a joyful occasion celebrated with a hearty meal of roast duck. Stefan's parents were now enjoying the beginning of their retirement in Frankfurt am Main, where they had settled along with many other young repressed Germans who had fled through Hungary for Austria at the end of the Cold War.

They referred to the Cold War as a time of 'persecution and espionage' and many still kept their old passports stamped by the Hungarian Border Service, as mementos of those years which forever changed both East and West Germany.

After graduating as an Engineer in Munich, Stefan had found work in this beautiful city where he now lived happily with Ayganysh.

The newlyweds had met four years ago during the city's annual Bavarian beer festival. Amidst the noisy bustle, Stefan and his friends noticed some lively, foreign students from the former Soviet Union, speaking in both Russian and German. The festival was the ideal place for students to meet each other and share common interests. It was also known as a perfect place to meet and date foreign students.

Stefan had smiled at the sight of the tall, moon-faced girl who was standing in front of him and furtively, kept glancing over to admire her slender physique, long brown hair and almond eyes. Ayganysh responded to his coy flirting by smiling at Stefan but due to his conservative upbringing and being afflicted by shyness since childhood, he was unable to approach her. They continued to exchange glances as the group of Russian-speaking students moved towards a long table to watch as waitresses competed against each other to carry six or seven enormous tankards of Bavarian beer. It was quite a spectacle to see these attractive, laughing girls wrestling with their foaming, overflowing vessels of one of Europe's most famous beverages.

The next day, Stefan had berated himself for not having spoken to Ayganysh and for a long time, felt completely lost and displaced. He had gone to work but did not hurry home. It was raining outside. Autumn is an amazing time in Munich with its tree-lined avenues ablaze with colour as the leaves turn. As he had walked alone, Stefan smoked and sang a soft melody to himself, sometimes moving as if dancing a waltz, oblivious to anyone around him. As people passed by, some understandably, shook their heads, whilst others looked at Stefan more sympathetically.

He had then been suddenly stopped in his tracks by a vision of those eyes that would forever conquer his heart! He was standing at the very place where he had first encountered that beautiful smile. He was talking to himself; uttering unrelated words that had meaning only for him. Stefan heard nothing, understood nothing. He was just walking through the rustling leaves against the sound of light drizzle.

"What's happening?" This question had been disturbing him for days, weeks, perhaps months. Time appeared to have stopped and nothing made any sense. He quietly whispered some verses he had recently read in a magazine by some little known poet who had died at the dawn of his creativity and in extreme poverty, whilst incarcerated in a psychiatric ward.

"Why had it taken so long for people to make sense of his poems? Are human hearts so cruel and cold that they were incapable of truly acknowledging his work when he was alive? How could it be that his visions and impulses were only now attracting the attention of readers?"

Thinking about the poet, Stefan had realised that he himself did not want to live for the rest of his days in exile from his own passions.

Could he be in love? His torn soul tossed and turned. Where should he look for her? How could he find her? He didn't even know her name! He lost his appetite, became emaciated, and he no longer had any interest in having fun with his friends.

"Is there a cure for this condition? This is nonsense!" Being in love is simply a chemical response in the brain!" No one else could help him deal with this ... Is this how he must now endure life? Is she, that moon-faced girl, his meaning in life? He was prepared to do anything, no matter how rash, just to see her again.

In the mornings, he found himself unwittingly pouring himself two cups of strongly brewed coffee. It was as though this mysterious girl with her sweet and gentle smile was constantly in his mind, night and day, wherever he went. He tortured himself with thoughts on how to find the girl. If she were the love of his life, they would surely meet some day.

Over and over again, he cursed himself loudly and mercilessly! He knew that he lacked a little determination and courage. Whether a result of the shortening days of autumn, his confused state or a combination of circumstances, he was unable to shake off his melancholy.

Stefan's boss, Mrs Ishma, was a plump woman in her fifties who wore a pinstriped suit. She was usually quite formidable but one warm, sunny day she approached Stefan and handed him the address and phone number of one of her friends. He was surprised and delighted since his boss's friend, Mrs. Kate, had a room to let in the area of the city that Stefan wanted to move to. After work, he slung his backpack over his shoulder and clasping his laptop, looked up the address. He was immediately excited to see that the studio room was on the top floor of a very large house with a magnificent façade. For young professionals working in Munich, it was rare and lucky to find such desirable accommodation and they normally had to settle for a cramped room in one of the students' apartment blocks.

How better to enjoy living in Munich; a city that young people subconsciously fall in love with and where they end up making their home? What kind of magic does this city hold for so many? Who knows? Perhaps it is the beautiful facades of its buildings and museums; or the story of King Ludwig, who built the nearby castle? According to legend, he lived in a fantasy world and dealt with the emptiness, by imagining a fictional court. It was said that his own uncle drowned Ludwig in the river, because of his unhealthy behaviour. The castle has fabulous views, as befitted its owner's taste and imagination. Its construction, which depleted the treasury at the time of its build, now generates a huge income for the whole of Bavaria.

Or perhaps it is the elegant streets, or the excellent beer, the unique smell and taste of which cannot be described in simple terms. Certainly, the annual beer festival attracts thousands of visitors and each year the number grows.

Mentally thanking his boss, Stefan slowly walked the last few metres up to the house but was suddenly overcome by a strange and inexplicable wave of emotion.

Regaining his composure, Stefan knocked at the door and was instantly mesmerized by the crystal voice of a young woman. When asked who was there and what he wanted, he replied that his boss had told him about the studio room for rent and he was interested in looking at it. The moments that followed were to prove the most marvellous and unforgettable of Stefan's life because when the door opened, standing before him, was the very same moon-faced girl he had seen at the Bavarian beer festival!

"Good evening"

Momentarily arrested by the sight of her almond shaped eyes and luxurious long brown hair, Stefan stood frozen at the door and the girl too, appeared to be caught in a sudden gridlock.

"Good evening" Stefan eventually managed to reply. He then inadvertently started his story again, "I was advised to come to this address to view the studio room which the landlady has to rent." He couldn't take his eyes off the girl for fear that she would once again disappear from his life, as he fumbled in his pocket for the note from Mrs. Ishma.

"Oh, I'm sorry! Yes, do come in." The girl smiled shyly at Stefan.

Entering the room where a few other viewers were gathered waiting to see the studio, Stefan still could not believe his luck in having the chance to become acquainted with Ayganysh, through her friend, his future landlady!

After viewing the room, he signed the rental contract, explaining that he was happy with everything and would even be able to walk to his office. Moreover, he agreed to move in immediately.

The sudden appearance of Stefan had both pleased and confused Ayganysh, who was far from immune to the admiring glances of this tall, young man with his cropped blond hair, dark brows and sparking blue eyes.

From the moment he moved in, Stefan wore an eternal smile on his face and found numerous excuses – the loan of salt for his evening meal, the request for sugar for his morning coffee - to call on Ayganysh. And so it was, that fate had decreed them neighbours; this handsome, 27 year old engineer and the moon-faced beauty with whom he had secretly fallen in love.

Before the winter break, Stefan plucked up the courage to invite Ayganysh and her friend for dinner and prepared a modest yet delicious meal. Anxious not to appear ignorant in conversations concerning her native land, he even researched the internet to become better acquainted with the mountainous country of Kyrgyzstan.

Stefan was surprised that from childhood, Ayganysh had dreamt of learning German and had nurtured an interest in German culture, history and daily life. Now that she lived in the country, she happily combined her day job at a geriatric nursing home with writing her thesis on the influence of oriental literature on western culture, in the evenings.

Ayganysh was totally captivated by her thesis and she and Stefan regularly spent long evenings discussing its subject matter, often returning to their rooms well after midnight.

Stefan was fervently and passionately in love. He still suffered from acute shyness, to the extent that he was sometimes unable to speak, but he soldiered on and continued to find any excuse to spend every free moment close to Ayganysh.

This was the manner in which they passed Munich's cold, winter days and since the continental frosts were long and hard there was still plenty of time until spring.

After the festive break, Ayganysh and her friend again gathered together with Stefan for discussions over a modest meal. Stefan was happy to try his hand at cooking, and by rejecting any help from the girls, he was able to abstract himself from their conversation whilst enjoying listening to what they had to say.

Stefan learned that Ayganysh had never seen her father. Her mum, formerly employed in scientific research, now taught in higher education. When the Soviet Union fell, people's lives changed dramatically and almost overnight, much was lost. Devaluation was immediate and as a result, many were plunged into poverty. The ideology, developed over a course of seventy years, appeared to turn to dust overnight. Scientific and Military Research projects were closed or simply transferred to Moscow. Most of the young scientists and intelligentsia travelled abroad. Huge holes were left in both society and the economy. Chaos continues even to this day...

Her mum, then a very young and beautiful woman, had lived with her parents who were both eternal optimists. Ayganysh's grandpa was often unwell and so her mother was torn between work and home. Sitting in the kitchen, Ayganysh now repeated her grandparents' favourite phrase: "Do you remember the old days, under the Soviet Union...?" prompting both girls to sarcastically mimic the facial expressions adopted by the older generation when they recounted happy memories of times past.

Time passed and February arrived.

One morning, clearly upset, Stefan went downstairs to see his neighbours and to give them his key. His grandfather had fallen very ill and he had to leave the city for a short while to visit him. Stefan had requested compassionate time off from his boss. Sympathetic and genuinely worried about Stefan's grandfather, Mrs. Ishma promised him paid leave and even offered to pay his travel expenses.

He was set to depart on Saint Valentine's Day, the date when in the midst of winter, young people throughout the world celebrate or hope to find love.

Ayganysh was upset to hear her beloved neighbour's news, especially when Stefan told her that he would be gone for about two weeks. It sounded like an eternity!

She wished him a safe journey then feeling a little lost, reluctantly got ready for work.

Finishing her hot chocolate, she sadly looked up at the ceiling. There was an unusual silence. Gone were the familiar morning sounds of Stefan getting ready for the day ahead.

As she made her way leisurely to the bus stop, Ayganysh had one hope and tearfully, allowed herself one wish "Let Stefan's grandfather recover so that once again I will hear our neighbour, my dear neighbour, in the morning."

Why, she wondered, did she long for Stefan to return quickly?

Ayganysh shrugged her shoulders and looked longingly at the windows of the flower shops with their special St Valentine displays of roses in every shade of burgundy, scarlet and red, and when she saw young couples embracing each other on every street corner and bus stop, her heart sank.

However, the holiday atmosphere in the nursing home where she worked soon lifted her mood. Arrangements had been made for the elderly to revisit memories of their youth. Everyone had dressed up and an old gramophone, along with 78 inch records of music fashionable in their heydays, had been sourced from the basement of a local five star hotel. The nursing home was one of the best in Germany and its excellent facilities and congenial atmosphere, meant that rich pensioners were prepared to wait for up to ten years for a room in this special place where they would end their days.

That evening, as she returned from work, Ayganysh was surprised to hear her mobile ring with a call from an unknown number but decided to answer it anyway.

"Hello, who is it?" She asked hesitantly

"Hello! Ayganysh, darling, how are you? Happy Valentine's Day!"

When she heard Stefan shouting down the phone, Ayganysh's heart almost leapt her chest and with tears of unexpected joy, she shouted back

"Stefan! Happy Valentine's Day to you too!"

She now found herself sobbing and didn't know what was happening to her.

"Ayganysh! Good news! My grandfather is much better so I'll be back in a couple of days. "Stefan sounded cheerful and optimistic

When the call ended, Ayganysh felt a rush of adrenaline surge through her body and holding the phone to her heart, she suddenly exclaimed, "Oh my God, I love him!"

She caught herself smiling constantly and alone on the street found herself dancing to a tune, which played in her mind.

Astonished by her feelings, Ayganysh felt as if she had stepped into a dream and doesn't every girl dream of love?

She was loved! And she was in love!

In addition, another surprise awaited her at home!

When her friend opened the door, she was thrilled to see the delivery of a vase of the loveliest red roses.

Ayganysh sat for a long time smelling and softly caressing the flowers, all the while smiling as tears of joy ran down her tender cheeks. She felt Stefan's presence beside her and closing her eyes, visualised her beloved: his shy smile, his jokes and his contagious laugh. Her heart sang and she knew that memories of this day would stay with her forever.

The heart of a girl is full of a mystique, power and tenderness, the personification of comfort and kindness.

How little it takes for a woman, when she is ready, to melt a man. How little a man or a woman needs to be truly happy!

On his return to Munich Stefan, asked Ayganysh to marry him and a modest wedding for close family and friends soon followed.

* * *

Chapter 10

Scotland, July 2014

The onslaught of a severe economic crisis in Europe led to chaos.

Germany managed to stay afloat but there were many redundancies. Stefan was lucky but found himself covering the workload of several positions which had been axed. Ayganysh took on a second job to help her young husband through that difficult period and her thesis was temporarily shelved, to be completed at a later date.

* * *

Their dream to travel to Scotland was postponed many times.

Every Friday night, Stefan 'dated' his beloved, young wife at the place where he had first declared his love for her and they often discussed their future and dreams of travelling the world. In a time of raging chaos, it was important that they did not lose sight of their plans and they both took heed of how those affected by the collapse of the Soviet Union had managed to survive and continue their lives with dignity.

They made plans, in spite of difficulties.

Love inspires those who know how to accept its gift.

So days, months and then two years passed, before Stefan and Ayganysh were finally able to transform their dream into reality.

* * *

They reached Belgium and then sailed by ferry to Edinburgh, Scotland's capital city. Feeling like pioneers, they continued their travels. It was an unusually hot July day and as a result, Stefan had to stop frequently to top up the water in the engine's cooling system. At times like these he often wished his studies in engineering had covered the basics of the internal combustion engine rather than silicon chips. Problems with the car continued and eventually they had to pull in at the side of the road. Many people stopped to assist but since it was a vintage model, none of the people in the passing cars were able to assist them.

Finally, a driver stopped to advise them of a nearby gathering of British vintage cars where hopefully, they would find someone with more specialist knowledge. Following his directions, Stefan and Ayganysh walked for twenty or thirty minutes to the site of the rally where, to their great relief, they discovered a collection of antique cars surrounded by crowds of enthusiasts, locals and tourists.

An elderly man with long whiskers and a distinct Scottish accent greeted them. As the organizer of the event, he knew a lot about vintage cars and told them that it would be his pleasure to have a look at their car.

As he drove them back to their vehicle, he chatted about life in his village and the forthcoming referendum, which if it resulted in Scotland becoming independent, would affect everyone in the country. The locals had been involved in lengthy discussions on the subject for several years and the majority was opposed to the proposed policy.

Many of the local industries had closed down or gone bankrupt and for a while, young people were forced to seek employment elsewhere. The economy had only recently started to recover and tourists were once again coming to visit Scotland's world famous natural and historic sites. This was much welcomed by small businesses in places, especially rural communities, which depended on tourism for revenue.

The Scottish National Party had long advocated separation but their ignorance of simple economic facts had spooked foreign investors. Many people were unhappy with the current political party's programme for development. The one thing that everyone longed for was stability, so they could live happily.

They discovered that this old man was a real patriot. He had lived through and survived many political changes in Britain. His father had fought in the First and Second World Wars, and born at the end of the war and growing up in the post war years, he had suffered both poverty and hunger. He enthusiastically told the young couple all about himself, his family, hobbies and what had inspired him to organize the vintage rally. He valued these old cars, not only for their beauty but also, for the human labour invested in their manual assembly.

The old man was indeed, very knowledgeable and having quickly diagnosed the problem with Stefan's car, he skilfully re-attached the cable to the heat sensor of the main engine block. There was however, a host of disconnected cables running all over the engine which he had never seen in such a vintage car. Whilst he could not see how they would affect the running of the engine, he came to the obvious conclusion that since they were there, he had better re-connect them. Thankfully German engineering ensured that each loose cable was only of a certain length and so each could only be fitted to a specific terminal.

After everything had been re-connected, Stefan turned the ignition key and the car jumped into life. The engine sounded sweeter than ever. "Maybe all those strange cables did have a function after all?" thought the old man, as he followed Stefan and Ayganish back to the car rally.

Entry to the event was free, to encourage people to come and admire these very rare vehicles, and when they returned to the site, Ayganysh and Stefan enjoyed looking around and taking photographs.

Before leaving, they thanked their rescuer sincerely for his invaluable, professional assistance and he in turn, was delighted to accept some beer which Stefan had brought from Bavaria.

Talking with the locals, the couple managed to discover a shorter route to their destination and climbing into their restored retro car, continued at full speed to the enigmatic Notrom Castle.

It was a magical place.

The site of the ruined castle was surrounded by a forest of spruce trees swaying gently in the summer breeze and the undergrowth concealed an abundance of wild mushrooms and berries, waiting to be gathered for a natural feast. Under the warm sun, two swans glided elegantly across a small pond, enjoying the cool water.

Stefan and Ayganysh felt as though they had entered a scene from a fairy tale and for a long time, stood enchanted by their surroundings.

Suddenly, the spell was broken by something unimaginable.

"My life has lost all meaning!"

With a piercing cry, an old man threw himself into the pond from the branch of a tree.

It was Rodgers! Dressed in clothes he had worn when he was young - a grey jacket, white shirt and a grey tie patterned with chess pieces and held with a clip - he had used a stepladder to climb into the tree. As he plunged beneath the surface of the water, the swans honked noisily, raising themselves out of the water and flapping their wings. They were clearly furious at being disturbed.

Ayganysh screamed in horror, clutching her mouth with her hands.

Without any hesitation, Stefan jumped in after the old man. Taking a deep breath, he dived under the water and grabbed the man's collar, then swam to the bank, dragging the man behind him.

This unexpected furore attracted the attention of other tourists and they rushed to the pond where a terrified Ayganysh was praying for her husband's safety.

"Leave me alone! I've made up my mind!

Spluttering, Rodgers tried to pull free of Stefan's grip.

"You're crazy!" shouted Stefan, spitting out water.

As he neared the shore, a couple of tourists helped pull both of them out whilst others ran to their tents for blankets and brandy. Each of them wanted to do something to help. Someone called the police and someone else told the ambulance that there were many victims. In short, panic reigned!

The old man, severely shaken with shock, looked angrily at his courageous rescuer. The thinning hair on his head was strewn with waterweed and he nervously squeezed at his wet tie as he sat shivering with cold.

Whilst Ayganysh helped Stefan change out of his wet clothes, everyone else speculated in hushed tones about the reasons for this strange old man's dramatic act. Kindly people tried to ask him about the whereabouts of his family and friends but Rodgers refused to respond either to them, the police or the ambulance crew. Despite his pleas to be left to his own devices, he was taken to a nearby hospital for checks on his mental health.

Once the excitement was over, the locals returned home, ready to continue life as normal without further thought of their neighbour's odd behaviour.

The sunset promised to be spectacular and looking forward to basking in its beauty and then welcoming the full moon, the tourists too, were determined not to dwell upon that afternoon's unfortunate incident.

Stefan and Ayganysh had pitched their tent in the camp where other young people were now busying about. Fires were lit and everyone settled down to eat and drink as they all waited for dusk to fall on the first of their three cherished nights in this enigmatic place.

* * *

Chapter 11

Foggy Hill Hotel, Scotland: Burns' Night, 25 January 2014

Burns' night usually coincides with winter's most severe weather. Snow lies thick on the ground and the biting wind tries to cut in half, anyone who ventures out on an evening walk.

It is a time when Scots organise recitals of their famous compatriot's poems, accompanied by a traditional supper of haggis; a humble dish to which Robert Burns famously dedicated one of his poems.

Despite his short life, the 18th century bard left a literary legacy, which is revered throughout the world; not least in Russia where translated by Samuil Marshak, Burns' poetic expressions of his liberal views, grows ever more popular.

Fred Rodgers remembered almost nothing about the last Burns' supper he attended.

The guest of honour had been the local laird; one of the richest landowners in Europe, well liked and respected by local farmers and the rural community for his generosity. A kindly man, he was always ready to support local events and often assisted individuals in times of hardship.

The local people embraced cultural events with great enthusiasm, eager to transfer their rich cultural heritage to future generations and to nurture new talent in all areas of the arts, especially Scottish poetry. On occasions steeped in Scottish history, and in particular Burns' night, they proudly donned the kilt.

Although recognised as Scotland's national dress, the origins of this garment – a long length of fabric wrapped around the waist like a skirt probably - belongs to Viking invaders. The Scottish kilt tightly pleated and woven in wool coloured with natural dyes, was warm, waterproof and adaptable and provided a form of camouflage. Over time, each clan developed their own tartans and often had one version for everyday wear and a second, more colourful, for formal wear.

That evening, Rodgers arrived in his kilt and after drinking several drams of whisky, was determined to convince his colleagues of his superior knowledge of Burns. He was particularly set on arguing his case to a neighbour, nicknamed 'chukhter', meaning highlander. The neighbour was a real Don Juan and he and his wife were the party's jovial hosts. He loved to joke with the women and now light-heartedly, entertained them with jibes against Rodgers. His most often used phrase came into play when he would meet a local lady and without any hint of sarcasm he would greet them with: "Oh, I almost didn't recognise you with your clothes on!" Rodgers just didn't like the chap and whilst pouring back the whisky, he inwardly vowed to put him in his place as soon as he started boasting about his knowledge of Burns.

By the time Rodgers rose to make his speech, he was seriously drunk and before he was even halfway through his opening salvo, he stumbled amongst the honourable guests. His jelly- like legs encountered a poorly placed chair and propelled forwards in some form of slow cartwheel, he ended up sprawled on the floor. And worst of all, as he performed his gymnastics, the full nakedness beneath his kilt became apparent to all.

The audience was appalled by what they had witnessed. Rodgers had literally fallen from grace.

Rodgers retired to the bar where he propped himself up on a stool beside one of the locals. Still drunk and feeling maudlin, he turned to the old man and launched into a rambling tale about his life. The story was full of inconsistencies and as he spoke about some maniac who had haunted him ever since he had failed on a mission, his eyes stared into the far distance. His face then became distorted as he nervously surveyed the room, as if expecting his predator to appear out of nowhere.

He was suspicious of everyone; convinced that anyone he encountered, even a villager, could be someone hired by that maniac. Shadows from the past lurked everywhere he looked, driving Rodgers to distraction.

Suddenly his face brightened as a memory of the tranquil years he had spent with his wife floated before his eyes. They had often come to this pub. A gifted musician, she had played the piano, and sometimes the organ at the local church, and a recollection of her masterful touch and evenings spent embracing each other as they danced to some romantic song, momentarily calmed Rodgers.

Since her death five years ago, Rodgers had suffered from loneliness and a sense of longing. He reproached himself for inwardly scolding her for leaving him all alone. He had hoped for a simple life with his wife by his side, where he no longer feared anyone or was compelled to fight for some elusive goal.

However, the rigid ideology of the Cold War remained firmly embedded in the minds of his fellow villagers. They still swore and raised their fists at the Russians and heartily condemned Communists. They were a product of their time: a period of contempt and hatred that had affected greatly the morale and mentality of their generation.

Now, everything was but a memory.

Nothing could be changed and the course of history could not be reversed.

They had lived their lives in fear through that century of chaos.

Now that his skills as a spy were no longer required, he felt disenfranchised. To whom could he reveal his feelings? Rodgers often thought about how 'cold shadows' are forced to live in their own dimension. Alone and wanted by no-one. He fancied that his fellow villagers knew about his past and quietly laughed at him.

Rodgers felt that he had been retreating into himself forever. Events that surfaced in his memory haunted him and carried him away.

The explosion of the Chernobyl Nuclear Power Plant had been unthinkable in both scale and its fatal consequences.

The strong radiation, carried by the wind and the rain from the crash site, destroyed much of the agriculture and livestock of Foggy Hill.

Some of the town's residents began to suffer from cancer and died young. His wife Lisa was one of them.

Farmers burned all the livestock that should have gone to market.

For a long time, people walked the streets wearing protective masks as if they were a fashion statement.

They often gathered in their deep basements in the belief that these were the only places which offered protection.

For the elderly in Foggy Hill, life became so monotonous that they felt as though time itself had been suspended.

There were three lovely ladies, however, who were exceptionally feisty. Their names were Heather, Lindsay and Cecile.

Rodgers had often been considered a match for Cecile, who lived next door to him, and it was from her that he had secretly stolen the wooden ladder for his sinister act.

Whenever he was very drunk, he used to pester her with seemingly nonsensical stories and considering him a nuisance, she would retreat to her cellar where donning her mask she would turn on the radio loudly to ward him off. Rejected, Rodgers would then return home, muttering:

"Even you are like a shadow to me."

All he had left were strong whisky and the relentless hallucinations in which some maniac pursued him.

And so, Rodgers planned to end his life. Drowning in a five-foot deep pond was clearly the only solution to all his problems.

* * *

Chapter 12

Notrom Castle, July 2014

In the dead of night, silence descended on the old castle. It was occasionally broken only by the faint croaking of frogs and the revellers' soft chatter and singing. Everyone who had stayed up to enjoy the magical spectacle of the full moon had returned to their tents. A gentle breeze wafted through the trees, whilst the swans slept soundly with their heads tucked neatly under their wings.

Stefan could not sleep. He had pitched their tent beside the place where the unfortunate Rodgers had tried to drown himself. Stefan quietly opened the tent flap and went out into the cool night air. As he walked to the water's edge he suddenly froze. Close to the pond, he noticed the shadow of a hunched figure quietly moving about, as though searching for something. The figure sat down for a second, dissolving into the darkness, and then illuminated by the bright moon, rose again so that Stefan was able to discern the features of the man's grinning face as he muttered:

"So, Rodgers: I've found you at last! I told you, you couldn't hide from me, you bastard!"

The man then wrapped something in a rag and disappeared.

It was all so unexpected, that Stefan could not decide whether it was real or if his mind were playing games on him.

He muttered under his breath: "Hmm, I wouldn't be surprised if there were strange ghosts wandering about this place."

Stefan returned to his tent and lay there breathing as slowly as he could. He thought, "Why did that shadowy figure suddenly turn up in this place? What is he up to? Who is this person?"

A slight noise next to his tent sent his heartrate into overdrive and he felt as if he could sense a human presence.

"Hm, how strange…" thought Stefan, as his heart pounded in his ears.

He turned to Ayganysh but she was sleeping soundly. He quietly got up, unzipped the tent flap and stepped out onto the cold grass. Stefan felt like his heart had stopped for several seconds when he realised that a human shadow was standing right beside him, breathing heavily.

Stefan could not see his face but he now felt a piece of cold steel pressing against his temple. A hand on his shoulder forced him to his knees and he squatted there not daring to move. Stefan slowly raised both of his arms in a show of surrender, despite having no real idea of what was happening to him.

The shadow whispered "Stand up but do not look at me and keep quiet."

"What a day! First some crazy old man tries to drown himself and now this?!" Stefan was totally confused and bewildered.

This deep voiced shadow lowered his gun and pulled from his pocket, a small torch and a piece of ragged material which he then slowly unfolded to reveal a tie-clip.

Stefan tried to follow the man's instructions and not look at his face but unable to resist, he raised his head and looked straight into the eyes of the 'shadow'. Adrenaline immediately surged through his body.

He would never forget those eyes – ice cold and dangerous. Stefan returned his gaze to the tie-clip and gave a straight answer:

"I don't know anything about this. I swear."

"Stop right there" growled his captor.

Stefan closed his eyes and in a controlled tone, continued: "I saved some old man today. I don't know who he was. He threw himself into the pond. He was taken to the local hospital" Stefan opened his eyes and felt a little braver.

Shultz didn't respond. He just smiled at Stefan and showed him a photograph which he had taken earlier of Stefan's car.

"If you will say anything to the police, I will find you. Don't try to be a dead hero. Remember that. Do you understand?"

Stefan slowly nodded his head.

Acute feelings of anger, fear and confusion raced through Stefan's mind. He had no idea how he had landed in this situation or how he should deal with it.

The figure then silently disappeared; it had emerged from nowhere and vanished just as suddenly. Stefan was left surrounded by the familiar sounds of the night - crickets and owls – and he shivered in recollection of what he had just experienced. It had been so surreal that it felt more like a horrible nightmare than reality.

He returned to his tent and quickly zipped up the flap with shaking hands but felt too anxious to sleep. The remainder of the night passed slowly and he only drifted off to sleep as the early morning sun glinted through the air vent of the tent.

When he eventually awoke the next day, Stefan resolved to say nothing of his night-time experience to Ayganish. He did not want to upset his wife since it was after all, their first holiday in three years. They spent the day exploring the castle and the surrounding woodlands and in the evening, listened to the campsite's musicians.

The magical mystique of the castle had been restored.

However, as soon as he went to bed, he was again tormented by memories of the previous day's events and his anxiety grew

Chapter 13

Foggy Hill Hospital, July 2014

The ambulance brought Rodgers to the local hospital where doctors concentrated on trying to stabilize him. Once the patient began to snore in his single ward, the doctors left their patient under the supervision of the nurse on night duty.

As he slept, Rodgers dreamt of Lauren, looking beautiful in a red dress within a vast space, empty apart from a grand staircase. These were sixty significant seconds of his life that haunted him day and night.

The memory that led him into the distant past, gave him the same clear picture, over and over again. He was suddenly struck by a fierce longing, buried deep in his heart for that woman from his past and felt young again.

He was smiling. If only he now could touch her and embrace her in a passionate kiss. He still wanted to satisfy his mad desire, after so many years. She would now be a mature woman but having also waited for true love, would give herself to him unconditionally. At times like these, his imagination encouraged him to rave as he dreamt.

as the night wore on. Stefan therefore determined that he had to remove Ayganysh from any risk of danger, real or imagined. Who knew when that shadowy figure might reappear and what impact it might have on their lives?

The following morning he gently awoke Ayganysh and told her that they were going home to Munich.

They had just finished packing up their tent when a police car, with siren wailing, came bumping along the track towards the castle grounds.

* * *

At some point, a pesky fly awakened him. He turned on the bedside lamp and for almost an hour, tried in vain to swat the fly with a folded newspaper.

A paramedic interrupted his fight: A paramedic who turned out to be none other than Schultz.

Their conversation was long and everything that had been kept secret for many years, now floated like a mirage in the desert.

Shultz now stood in front of him, like a cold shadow from the past, gazing at Rodgers whilst smoking the last cigarette from his pack.

Rodgers sat for a long time, showing no emotion apart from raising his eyebrows and occasionally averting his gaze from the man to the view outside the window.

It felt like all of his hopes and dreams, bound in his 'heroic' act of leaping into that ill-fated pond, had dissipated in the worst way possible.

This was the dreaded liaison that he had tried so hard to avoid by the action taken at the pond. Now, here they were, staring at each other with eyes sparkling and clenched teeth. Tangled in intrigue, they were caught in a big web, like objects being cleverly manipulated in someone's game.

The picture became clearer, more or less.

"There was nothing between us, I swear!" Rodgers muttered. Surely, the man who was challenging him would realise that their colleagues would have noticed any clandestine meetings or dates between Rodgers and this woman. Rodgers sensed that Schultz had guessed what he harboured in his innermost thoughts, down to the smallest details of his illusions.

He grew very afraid.

"I know that you were attracted to her." Schultz quietly continued, pursing his lips. He then pulled from his pocket, a piece of cloth that contained the tie clip that had fallen to the ground when Stefan pulled Rodgers ashore. Shultz threw it on the bed.

It was worse than a nightmare.

Realizing that this villain, this cold and emotionless spy, had come to destroy all that related to his past, including all of his fond memories, Rodgers shouted at Schultz, deliberately provoking a response.

"Schultz, you must have known that she never loved either you or me."

"How could you know that?" Shultz started to lose patience.

"You see, she's not with me, Schultz."

Rodgers was no longer afraid. If he took a bullet to his forehead, he knew that his passion and his memories would remain with him and him alone.

"You'd like that to be the case, wouldn't you Rodgers?"

Schultz's face reddened, his male pride clearly wounded but male pride, clearly wounded, but Rodgers immediately retorted:

"We were both tortured by unrequited love for this woman."

Even as Rodgers spoke of her, a warm feeling surged within him and he hoped that somewhere, far away, she had at last found happiness after all she had suffered. However, his words only served to further exacerbate the situation.

Schultz finished his cigarette and softly whispered:

"Every risk and heroic act I ever took, were for her alone! Yet you choose to mock me like the idiot you are!" Clenching his teeth, he slowly pulled a pistol from his inner coat pocket and pointed its silencer at Rodgers.

"Go ahead and shoot me, Schultz, but you'll never know where she is." Rodgers continued to taunt him, without fully realizing the danger he was in.

Suddenly a bullet splattered Rodgers' brain over the walls of the ward.

Schultz surveyed the scene and then silently walked undetected, out of the hospital.

As he made his way to his car, he pulled a photograph from his pocket with the image of a number plate of another car. It was Stefan and Ayganysh's vintage VW. He stopped and stared at it and then carefully replaced it.

If Rodgers had not been involved in the failure of the operation, then who was? Who had taken his wife?

He took a deep breath, ready to take a step closer to achieving his goal.

He remembered the day when the documents had gone missing and had no regrets about strangling the Russian professor's wife who had given him the wrong papers. He had then concluded that it had been Rodgers with whom Lauren had disappeared, along with the highly prized, authentic research documents.

Schultz had no other option but to find his wife, Lauren; the woman who had betrayed his feelings, his love and his hope.

How he longed to find her and escape with her to the edge of the world, the North Pole, where she would belong only to him. He dreamed of an innocent life where he and his beloved would sit and enjoy the Northern lights. He envisaged their touching beauty, far from this desert where everything was alien and cruel. Sometimes even Schultz craved the innocent happiness of a child and when excited by the prospect, was propelled to take erratic action. He believed that his motives justified his actions, and made decisive plans to win back Lauren.

Schultz did not want to acknowledge how insidious, even poisonous, his love had become. He liked to control her every move, to hound her, and predict her desires. He kept in his memory her every breath, her every glance. He might have felt belittled and made to look stupid, but he was willing to forgive her everything to resume a normal life.

After the unfortunate affair, created only in his own imagination, he assumed that his endeavours to catch her would lead to a stunning and phenomenal success!

He was a true predator. He was determined to hunt down his wife wherever she was and regardless of whom she was with.

His head was now full of confused thoughts. Why wasn't his wife with Rodgers, after flirting so blatantly with him? Had she not dared to run away with him?

"Had she used Rodgers, just like she used me?" The very thought filled Schultz with disgust.

Schultz grew even angrier. He started to scroll through his memory all over again. He recalled Lauren's every move. What details had he missed to lead him to pursue this loser, Rodgers, who turned out to be a pawn in some other game? Lauren knew exactly what she was doing, by staying in touch with Schultz and Rodgers. She clearly had a specific plan.

So if she'd chosen neither Schultz nor Rodgers, who was she with now?

Moaning and seething with jealous rage, he began to pace to and fro like a caged animal.

Had she ever really loved Schultz? Or had he dreamt it? Perhaps his selfishness had made him blind to reality? Maybe…

"Oh, Lauren! Lauren!" shouted Schultz.

He had first met Lauren at a bustling party. Amidst the surrealist atmosphere of their work with its high risks and dangerous missions, these parties were considered special; somewhere they could all let down their hair and feel like ordinary people. They offered a welcome distraction and encouraged relaxed conversation around common interests, hobbies and places where they socialised. These parties were like pieces of bright and surrealistic dreams.

Spies tried to pretend they had normal lives but only some of them succeeded.

In contrast with that what happened in reality, these parties had their own weird and sometimes intriguing, implications. On that particular evening, Schultz had arrived a little late but as soon as he walked in through the door, he saw Lauren. From then on, his eyes remained glued to his dream woman.

She had been going upstairs from the ground floor and he had noticed her long, slender fingers with their dark maroon nails, holding the banister. She had then turned to wave at someone. Was that gesture made to the third person in the equation?

She smoked a long, thin cigarette and in her red dress and retro hairstyle, looked like a character from a film. As music played softly in a corner, she approached Schultz with a radiant and charming smile and as she sipped her French red wine, began to flirt cutely with him.

For Schultz, these moments seemed the most magical and alluring of his life. They inspired him and gave him wings. The meaning of his life changed forever.

From that moment onwards, each new risk he faced, he dedicated to her.

He now knew what he strived for and did everything in his power to draw her attention. He would be the best and most revered spy; someone with whom she would feel valued as a woman and behind whom she could hide from this insane and terrible world!

"A man should love passionately, with the instinct of an animal" Schultz told himself. This would prove to be the most dangerous and impulsive game of their lives but he thrived on the adrenaline flowing through his brain and relished the role of being a real hero in her eyes.

Such feelings only existed when he was with her.

Without her, he would feel nothing.

Now, as he sped down the highway, he searched his mind for the thread which linked Lauren with a stranger.

Who was he? Who was the bastard who had stolen his prey from under his nose?

* * *

Those early years…

It was the quiet and warm month of October. Lauren was going to spend the weekend in a small apartment in the centre of Brussels. She was already on her way when she received a message from Schultz, asking her to wait for him at the country park near the border between France and Belgium.

It was rather strange that Schultz had appointed that particular place to meet her. He seemed to know exactly where she was going. She pulled up in the designated car park and got out of her car. She looked around and stretched, deeply inhaling the fresh air. It had been a long time since she had been at one with nature and standing beneath the clear blue sky, she closed her eyes and with outstretched arms, immersed herself in the silence.

Suddenly she heard a sharp rustling sound as a flock of birds took to the air from the nearby lake. Lauren stiffened. As soon as she stepped to the side of the car, a shot rang out like a thunderbolt. The bullet shattered the car's windscreen. Lauren turned and took the only escape open to her by jumping into the lake and swimming towards a thick clump of reeds.

As she looked back, four men appeared out of a thicket of sea buckthorn, armed with long hunting rifles. They looked like genuine hunters but as they approached the car and then the lake, it was clear that these people had not come to shoot ducks.

Their target was Lauren.

With the unexpected attack by the ferocious hunters, she had become an unwitting victim and was now trapped.

Keeping the reeds between herself and the hunters, Lauren swam underwater for as long as possible, emerging only to draw breath and to assess the situation. There was nothing she could do but try to escape the hunters by any means possible.

She had no idea who was attacking her or why, but her instinct to flee her pursuers and save her life was strong.

The men had spread out to continue their chase and Lauren, despite her athletic training, was growing exhausted. She felt confused by the unexpected attack but in desperation, quickly harnessed her remaining strength and once again dived below the surface, determined to swim to the other side of the small lake. Even underwater, she heard the shot and this time felt the bullet graze the delicate skin of her exposed shoulder. In severe pain, she dived deep, chastising herself for not having picked up her loaded gun from the car.

Lauren had been returning from a special assignment in Paris. The mission had been a complete success and she had no conflicts with the French Secret Service, so who could be shooting at her? She had only stopped at this place for what was supposed to be a romantic rendezvous.

Lauren quietly surfaced from the shallows near the edge of the lake, moaning softly as she clutched her wounded shoulder. She sipped some fresh air. She could no longer swim underwater but realised that she had to keep her head low and remain unseen. Otherwise, she would get a bullet to her forehead. Her head was spinning. Suddenly, she heard the sound of the men approaching from amongst the reeds on the bank.

What should she do? Her wounded shoulder had now become numb, making it difficult to swim.

Lauren understood nothing. Would she die here, under these most absurd circumstances, without having completed the most important mission of her career?

There must be an end to this unexpected nightmare. Where was Schultz? Had he forgotten about their meeting? She had only recently decided, after much deliberation, to commit to a serious relationship with him. Schultz's persistence had won her over.

"Oh, Schultz, where are you?"

She knew that if she raised her head even a few centimetres, this time, the killers wouldn't miss. She heard their voices rise in agitation as they discussed something in French. It was an easy translation:

"Damn! He owes us a lot of money! Where is he?"

Lauren grew even more confused:

"What money? Who were they waiting to pay them; and for what?"

She heard two shots. A few moments later, two more shots rang out. Then everything fell silent and she noticed Schultz crawling out of the reeds. He immediately swam towards her and hugging her gently, helped her swim to the bank.

As Schultz pulled her ashore, Lauren almost passed out with both pain and shock, whilst desperately trying to fathom what linked her pre-arranged meeting with Schultz and the unexpected attack from those deranged hunters.

Schultz was very gentle with her as he bandaged her wounded shoulder. She was now completely under his protection.

She asked him nothing but questions raced through her mind.

"Why was he so late? Who were these men? Why did he owe them money?"

Lauren could not fathom out what was going on.

She was however, safe for the time being and would now be able to complete the most important mission of her life.

As for Shultz; he was obviously not who he claimed to be.

She lay on the grass, shivering with cold and pain, with her still wet clothes clinging to her young, svelte body. Her shoulder straps had torn and her dress had slipped down exposing her breasts and pink nipples.

Schultz could not take his eyes off Lauren.

Lauren hugged him tightly in gratitude as she cried heavily through chattering teeth.

The beauty and grace of the female body can be spellbinding and Schultz was momentarily mesmerised before coming to his senses and wrapping her in his sweater.

The warm light of that autumnal evening which gave a natural lull to the atmosphere of this wonderful place, coupled with the woman's sensuous, naked body, filled him with anticipation of romance. The sun sank gently behind the hill, illuminating the colourful splendour of the trees' autumnal foliage. Tomorrow would be another beautiful day.

Meanwhile, Schultz collected dry branches and lit a fire. Its amber hues played upon her slender neck, rising upwards to her blond hair and grey eyes. Her every breath and luscious lips fuelled Shultz's passion.

He tenderly kissed her and stroked her alluring nakedness and she gave herself to him completely. Schultz felt as if this was the moment he had been waiting for all of his life. He took an avid enjoyment in his lovemaking with the woman for whom his passion would be eternal.

He knew that at last, he had found something that would provide a safe haven from the world's chaos and the dangerous missions and intrigues of his work. He had someone to return to, safe and sound.

Schultz asked Lauren to marry him straight away and when she enthusiastically accepted without hesitation, his feelings of joy pushed all reservations about other matters to the back of his mind.

When I awoke from a deep sleep,
I was again plunged into a state of bliss
I escaped an empty existence.
When I heard the song of an angel
And looked into the eyes of
The one whom I had been seeking
Each spring and early morning.
I was mute, I was blind,
I was only half alive
You breathed hope into me
As you shyly bent towards me,
Delicate shoulders, hidden
Beneath your wet hair
Your every breath
I kept treasured in my memory
Ready to dispel
An empty existence.
I was devoured by brutal guilt.
As I lay helplessly,
And without hope at the rock,
I realized that I had lost you forever.
I whined loudly at the moon,
I longed to touch your lips
And again, taste their sweetness,
Your passion filled me with hope
Giving me wings and space to breathe
In this vast emptiness

You left only a thin thread
For me to cling to
And protect me against loneliness
I never lost hope that
You would emerge from my dreams
I would be ready to
Conquer the world for you.
I made a vow to myself.
That I would navigate the clouds
To find you
As you fluttered from sight
Only then would
Your exhausted prisoner be freed
From his confinement
To an empty existence.

* * *

Chapter 14

Shultz

Such was his passion for her that he agreed to travel to Kyrgyzstan, risking everything, including his life.

This deceptively straightforward mission carried the danger of fatal consequences but also offered high financial reward which would allow him to retire and dedicate his life only to her. The essence of the operation was to infiltrate the domain of a certain professor who was working on a secret project. Several special services were seeking to steal his work.

Schultz was a tall, athletic man. His broad black eyebrows were set in a permanent frown and his distinctive facial features - his wolverine eyes, the sharp contour of his nose and angular jaw - expressed his strong-willed, yet intolerant, personality. People who fell under Schultz's intense stare would never forget it.

Their time together turned out to be limited. News had reached him that critical data had been accessed by another organisation and it was imperative that he immediately determined a means of gaining advantage.

On the eve of his departure he treated Lauren to a romantic dinner, with the promise that this would be his final mission.

Thereafter, they never would be apart.

Buoyed by his trust in his wife and with the revelation that he was ready to sacrifice everything for her, he told her that after this operation, they would disappear somewhere where no-one would find them. They would be fabulously wealthy and he would give her the world.

Lauren appeared particularly beautiful to Schultz and sweeter and more playful than usual on their last evening together. The following day, Schultz opened his eyes to see Lauren standing at the window with a cup of coffee and a cigarette in her hand. The morning sun lightly touched her snow-white, tender skin, celebrating her femininity. Schultz raised his head then leant back on the pillows to continue admiring her.

Lauren seemed oblivious to his gaze. She was standing half-turned, with one leg slightly bent. Her translucent, white peignoir had fallen from her shoulders, exposing her neck and back, as her perfectly manicured, long, slender fingers tapped on the window sill, as if playing a piano.

Schultz would never forget this image of Lauren.

She turned around and smiled when she saw that Schultz was awake. Her glance however, felt somewhat alien and disturbed something deep within Schultz. His heart sank with the knowledge that very soon he would be forced to be apart from her for a long period of time.

What if they never saw each other again? What if he were now seeing Lauren for the last time?

"Damn it! What nonsense!" Schultz got up and sat on the edge of the bed, staring at himself in the mirror.

Of course, he didn't want to leave her. He especially didn't want to leave her alone, knowing that Rodgers was around. Even the thought of that loser talking to her, filled him with rage.

Sparring partners of old, they had again crossed each other the previous day as the final phase of this operation was to involve both of them and they were briefed together. Rodgers had been sarcastic as usual. It had become a habit.

Rodgers had started it:

"Doesn't Lauren see what a crazy lunatic you are?"

After trying to evade the issue, Schultz then launched a counter attack:

"And what makes you think that you are more deserving of her attention?"

In a volley of punches, he struck Rodgers in the kidneys and without waiting for his opponent's recovery, hurried to meet his beloved.

Rodgers was winded for a while but he was not going to give up. He had already tried on several occasions, to confess to his wife that he loved another woman. His wife had guessed but firmly kept her silence. It would have been easier for her to receive news of his death than give him a divorce. Poor Rodgers had no idea that Schultz and Lauren had now secretly married.

And Schultz, more than anyone else, was convinced of his superiority.

"Lauren, you'll remain true to me, I know. What is Rodgers? Mediocre!! You are mine and only mine"

Still looking at his reflection, Schultz prided himself on how good and courageous he looked.

It was an image that would prove very useful in the implementation of his forthcoming mission.

He already knew how to best secure a quick and satisfactory outcome to the operation. According to information received, he had to gain the trust of one scientist and then steal the documents from his laboratory.

Schultz also was aware that the scientist's spouse was a housewife and new to a foreign city, had not made many friends. According to descriptions of her character and judging by her photos, it would not be difficult to make her his accomplice.

A plan of action had been drawn up but as an experienced spy, he knew that he might have to respond to a change of circumstances.

He had to go. He had no choice but to perform this mission but on his return, Schultz was determined to disappear with Lauren forever. He was sure that he would be rich; fabulously rich.

Schultz pulled his wits together and approached Lauren. She was slowly putting on her stockings. He hugged her and squeezed her in his arms.

Should we stay obedient to our souls?
And feel pleased by what fate has given us?
Don't try to find a formula for love
The Ocean will sing you a silent serenade.
Promising that even if you plunge to its depths
You can ascend again, in new directions
All obstacles are of your own invention
Your sudden sigh shows that you have everything you want
If only for a moment
And that moment will change your path for eternity
The stars of the Milky Way which seduced you
Will return you to me in a new light.

* * *

Cold Shadows

Chapter 15

Highway. Scotland

Schultz suddenly stopped the car and got out, gasping for breath. He looked pale and felt awful.

He recalled the case of the hired 'farmers' who were supposed to scare Lauren by chasing her, so that Schultz could then come to her rescue and in her eyes, become her hero. His plan was supposed to have been foolproof. He had promised money to those poor fellows for their innocuous role and they had happily agreed to play along, not realizing how this poor joke on the vulnerable girl would turn out.

Schultz had never imagined that he would end up a puppet, controlled by the hands of someone else.

Leafing through Rodgers's diary, he found a short article which had been torn from an old French newspaper. It reported the case of four local farmers who had disappeared without trace. Although the previous investigation into their whereabouts had been closed, the article called for any new evidence that would allow the local police to re-open the case.

Schultz held his head in his hands, infuriated by how blind he had been.

How had Rodgers come across this article and why had he kept it? What did he know about these men's 'disappearance'? Was he the third party in the equation, after all? No longer alive, he could say nothing on the matter but despite being dead, he could still have left behind more secrets than Schultz imagined.

On that day by the lake, as soon as Schultz realized that Lauren had been wounded, something immediately clicked in his brain and he had automatically grabbed his gun and fired at the hunters in the reeds.

He fired only two shots. The bogus hunters hesitated but had already raised a noisy alarm. Schultz had then raced to the other side of the lake, where he expected to find them.

He heard two more shots and when he discovered four corpses, began to call Lauren. She quietly let out a groan. Schultz, raking through the reeds with his hands, shoulder-deep in water, found his beloved and hugging her tightly against him, swam to the shore.

At the time, he was in no doubt that it had been Lauren who had shot the other two hunters. He had decided that she must have dropped her gun into the lake after being hit by a bullet.

Schultz had put her in the car and driven straight across the field, keeping up the presence that he was rescuing her from unknown enemies. After a few miles he drew up beside a large tree, close to a private hotel; a charming dwelling built in the local Baroque style. As soon as they entered, the owner noticed Lauren's bleeding shoulder and producing a first aid kit, suggested that he call an ambulance. Schultz thanked him for his offer but assured him that since he was a doctor, he would treat her himself. He then pulled out a syringe and gave her a couple of shots before cleaning her wound, which fortunately proved to be little more than a minor graze.

The owner hesitated and then asked what had happened. He was told that Lauren had been swimming in the lake and had accidently become ensnared in the reeds which grew densely along its banks.

Schultz ordered a couple of stiff drinks and began to plot his next move. He would need to collect Lauren's car in order to destroy all evidence of their being at the lake. His beloved's car could not be detected or touched by anyone.

Returning to the lake, Schultz first rushed to the place where the dead hunters had lain but to his astonishment, the bodies had disappeared.

Who could have got rid of them before Schultz arrived at the scene? Who could have known about this unfortunate undertaking except for him and Lauren?

Was it Rodgers? Did he have an accomplice?

And when he retrieved her car, he found her pistol securely lodged in its secret compartment. More questions flooded through his mind.

He could not say anything to Lauren, since he'd promised that he would take care of everything. Early in the morning after strong coffee, he delivered her car and after their honeymoon, sent her back to Budapest.

Schultz now urgently needed to know who was playing with them and who had destroyed all of the evidence, including the bodies of the four, unfortunate hunters. Who was the third man? Who was this invisible person who knew of Schultz's plans, and indeed his thoughts, in advance?

Following the incident with the dangerous hunters, Lauren had never left his side. So it was evident that someone was keeping watch over Shultz. The third man? Who was he? Could it be Rodgers? Certainly, he would have had a strong motive. No, it was impossible! At the time, he had been away, intent on divorcing his wife so that he could offer his hand to Lauren. And his diary, despite being poorly scrawled in French, confirmed his where-abouts and innocence.

By using his contacts and because he had knowledge of Rodgers' itinerary and could thus map out his every move, Schultz could easily frame him but time was running out and he now had his own important mission to accomplish; a potentially dangerous situation which involved them both. And this would provide Schultz with the perfect explanation for Rodgers' demise: he would simply claim that Rodgers had not survived.

So the identity of the third protagonist remained a mystery.

But wait! He once again mentally scrolled through scenes from the party, concentrating on everyone who was there. The staircase! As Lauren climbed the stairs, she had waved to someone standing in the dimly lit area at the far side of the room.

Try as he might, through a process of elimination, Schultz could not identify who this had been. There was however, one employee, who rarely appeared on campus. He was quietly sociable and got on well with his colleagues but to Schultz's knowledge his conversations with Lauren did not extend beyond niceties such as: "How is your family?" or "What's new, Mademoiselle?" He had spent quite a long time at the party but then disappeared and had not been seen for some time. Their paths never crossed at work. Was he the one behind all of this?

At first, Schultz dismissed the notion but thinking back, he grew more convinced. For a start, the moustache sported by that man had certainly looked false! When he had encountered Schultz at the party, he had been quick to turn away, giving a little nod to Lauren before moving to the quiet side of the room.

Schultz hadn't given this man a second thought. His attention was focused exclusively on Lauren and he recalled how irritated he had been by her flirting with drunken Rodgers, when all he wanted to do was kiss her hands and whisper sweet nothings in her ear.

Schultz dragged on his Chesterfield cigarette, leaning against his car on the North Sea coast.

A warm breeze gently stroked Schultz's curly hair.

As he looked skywards, the stars seemed to fade away one by one and the moon assumed a more leaden and callous face. Such moments, caught between the darkness of the night and the weak early morning light, had always felt special to Schultz. The presence of the white globe suspended in the sky made him feel reborn.

His mind was in turmoil. And he was shocked to the core by the realisation that this alternative mission had been clearly planned and indeed led, by his wife Lauren and her unknown accomplice in his lazy disguise.

"Bastards!" He let out a mighty roar.

Schultz could not help but try to dismiss from his mind, what now seemed obvious. He did not want to believe that he had been beaten. So the third man had been an accomplice of Lauren's. Perhaps he had even been her lover, that impudent creature who had ruined his very important mission? And she, his wife, had informed him of Schultz's every move. Before he and the Russian scientist's wife had boarded the train and prior to their arrival in Moscow, Schultz had twice rechecked the contents of the stolen briefcase, to ensure the authenticity of the classified material and yet somehow, Lauren and that young devil with the moustache, had managed to replace it with bogus documents.

Schultz had left the carriage for a smoke and as he stood in the corridor, reconsidered his plan on how to remain as inconspicuous as possible. An elderly couple in the next carriage had shown some interest in his companion, the unhappy wife of the professor, and Shultz had made sure that he was always by her side pretending to be an attentive lover, to prevent her from engaging in conversation with them.

As the journey had progressed, he had ensured that the door to their compartment remained locked, especially when the train stopped at stations, and had warned the Conductor in advance, not to disturb them.

His plan was clear. Before reaching Moscow, he had to take his briefcase and hide in the compartment where the driver and controllers rested and prepared tea for passengers. As soon as all the passengers had disembarked, he had to change into a train driver's uniform and then leave the train, unnoticed. He would then have no further need of the professor's crazy wife who had fallen so fervently and passionately in love with him.

Schultz could never have anticipated the final outcome of their journey: that his whole mission would collapse as the result of the exchange of documents and the unexpected tantrum of the professor's wife which led to him strangling her in a fit of rage.

But who had replaced those documents and when? Could it have been the Conductor who paid such close attention to his tie? Or the elderly married couple? Were they all accomplices of Lauren's? Impossible!

Schultz continued to rage aloud and tore at his hair.

We're all cold shadows in this life!

"I failed! No, no way!

Lauren! I loved you! I still love you! Ah, Lauren!"

He jumped into the sea. The water was cold and he swam to both cool down and reorder his thoughts. Suddenly, he felt a strong scalding sensation as something whipped against his legs and shoulders. The water was full of small jellyfish but already far from shore, he had no choice but to endure their terrible stings until he reached the beach.

Damn it! This was the final straw which heightened his determination to seek vengeance for all that he had experienced after his failed mission!

Schultz could not return to the organization without those critical documents. The findings of the scientist and the discovery of their disappearance would further strengthen the hostility between the countries maintaining the arms race. The prevention of peace negotiations was the main goal of the organization. And they had earned fortunes from it.

Schultz had dreamt about how he and Lauren would live happily and financially secure into their old age, fleeing far away to the North Pole. But this ominous day and his failed mission had given birth to a new and more dangerous predator. He was now on the run from everyone, including himself!

In his mind, he replayed that day's events yet again and was suddenly hit by a sickening realization.

Oh my God!

The driver of that car, that insolent, young, lean 'man' had been Lauren! She had been well disguised but the eyes, those beautiful grey eyes, could not be confused with anyone else's. Why hadn't he paid more attention at the time?

Because, it had simply been inconceivable!

Her execution of this counter mission had been almost flawless! A wild and nasty grin spread over Schultz's face. Recognizing how truly inept he had been, he grew even angrier and plunged again and again below the waves as if trying to purge himself of his past.

However, memories continued to pound at his temples. He was not the perfect spy that he considered and imagined himself to be. He was a loser: a mere pawn in someone else's more sinister and accomplished game.

Lauren had never belonged to him and it was this which tormented him the most. He shouted and swam shaking off the seaweed that clung to his body like his rotten past. He couldn't accept the truth.

Schultz revisited a long sought fantasy. For many years, he had romantically visualized Lauren sitting on the shore, waiting for him alone, as if caught in a scene from an old black and white film. Her anxious face, his longing for affection and love, had left a deep impression as he pictured them communicating without any need for words.

Now this image brought only mental torture, sullied by his regrets and disappointment in himself.

Schultz felt totally worthless.

Above all, he was angry with himself. Deep down, he knew that the thought of her suffering aroused in him, a sense of power and control. He also knew that despite the anger he felt towards her, he could not face life alone.

Schultz eventually swam ashore. He sat for a few minutes to dry off then found his clothes and dressed. As he pulled on his jeans he took the car key out of the pocket and threw it as far as he could into the sea.

After a long wait by the side of the road he managed to hitch a lift into Edinburgh. As he made for his hotel he was suddenly struck by a fit of vomiting brought on by the jellyfish stings. He retraced his steps to a NHS clinic he had noticed in passing, and was immediately given an analgesic to boost his system.

As he flopped down on the bed of his executive suite in the Capital's prestigious Sheraton Hotel to recuperate, he flicked on the TV. A very familiar young German was being interviewed by a

BBC correspondent and was recounting his experience at Nortom Castle the previous day. Red mist descended over Schultz's eyes then recognition kicked in: the green car behind the young German, glistening in the daylight, took Schultz straight back to one particular day in Budapest.

A sudden sense of connection lifted his malaise and he pulled out the picture of the old VW car's registration plate and fed the details to his contacts in the Organization. He then carefully reworked his appearance and after falsifying his passport, left Edinburgh's Sheraton hotel without a trace. He hailed a taxi and set off for the airport without wasting any more time. As he sat in the back of the taxi, a text message came through on his phone. He booked himself onto the next flight to Munich.

* * *

Chapter 16

Leaving Scotland

The sun rose, generously spreading its rays over the limitless blue sky. Dawn was cloudless, promising good weather for the whole day. Tourists waiting for the ferry stood in the sunshine beside their cars until one by one, they filed into the vast cavern of the lower car deck.

Stefan and Ayganysh managed to park their old car in the farthest corner then quietly slipped unseen, off the ferry and back to shore.

"Ayganysh, we are not sailing on the ferry. My heart tells me that something is wrong." Stefan announced seriously after considering an alternative to returning by ferry.

Early that morning the police had arrived at the pond and assuming that they had come to find out more about Rodgers' attempted suicide, the young people engaged them with tales of how Stefan and a couple of tourists had rescued him from drowning.

Stefan and Ayganish had been interviewed at length by the police and then even more thoroughly by a posse of eager journalists. They had even endured having make- up applied before being interviewed on TV during which Stefan had studiously recounted how he had saved Rodgers from his attempted suicide in the little pond.

The purpose of their visit however, was far more sinister. The police were now looking for Rodgers' murderer. A cleaning lady had raised the alarm when she discovered Rodgers' body in the hospital earlier on and the night watchman had been so traumatized by the terrible scene that he had collapsed on the floor.

The paramedic listed as being on duty was nowhere to be found - neither in the hospital nor at the address where he allegedly lived.

Nothing showed up on the security system. The CCTV footage was blank. There were no records of anyone entering or leaving the building, or the true identity of the paramedic.

The night watchman had seen nothing but as a prime suspect, was arrested and taken in for questioning before being released. He dimly recalled seeing a strange man hovering around the hospital corridors in the afternoon and remembered that he had periodically looked into the room where Rodgers, heavily sedated, was asleep. He hadn't seen him again during the evening but was able to provide the police with a description of the stranger's general appearance and facial features.

Everyone staying at the old castle was questioned and once the police were satisfied that no-one had seen the man in the iden tikit image drawn up from the night watchman's description of the stranger, surrounded the pond with yellow tape. All of the young revellers, who only the night before had basked in the magical atmosphere of this special place under the glow of the full moon, were immediately ushered off the site.

Broadening their search, the police later found a paramedic's gown and an abandoned rental car on the shores of the North Sea, some distance from the castle.

There was little else to go on since the car hire company confirmed that the vehicle had been rented out to an elderly woman.

There was however, one witness. A fisherman, who had been fixing his boat's engine early in the morning, had seen a mature, and strongly built, half-naked man swimming and yelling near the shore. However, when he had tried to get a closer look, the man, like a ghost, had disappeared.

* * *

Stefan paused and turning to Ayganysh he began his rehearsed story "We'll travel by plane. I've already booked the tickets. The ferry will take our car. Stay close to me."

"That first night at the castle when everyone went to their tents, I couldn't sleep and so lifted our tent flap to get some fresh air. The moon was still bright and I saw a shadow flash by and then reappear not far from our tent. It hovered about like a ghost and appeared to have found something on the spot where you helped the old man change his clothes. Then the shadow quietly disappeared. Over and above all these interviews with the police, I feel that we've become embroiled in some kind of mess, which I can't explain for the time being."

"Stefan, I've never felt so scared. Why didn't you tell the local police? And now, you're burning up." - Ayganysh replied anxiously, touching Stefan's burning cheeks. Stefan felt a little guilty about only recalling part of what had happened but he wanted to protect her from the truth until he knew more about the cause of the incident.

They waited until the ferry sailed, then took a taxi to Edinburgh Airport.

On the way, Stefan repeatedly tried to reach their landlady by calling, texting and leaving messages for her to contact them, but she didn't pick up the phone or text back. It all felt very ominous and Stefan grew increasingly anxious about both Mrs Kate and Ayganysh's roommate.

* * *

Chapter 17

Moscow – Frunze, Mid -1980s

The chemist Stanislav Petrovich Komarov lived and worked in Moscow but because he had been instructed by the Committee for Special Affairs to undertake a more complex task, it was necessary for him to travel to Frunze. He had no choice. His mission was to establish a new laboratory in the Kyrgyz capital city and to explore the mineral composition of the rich resources of underground water and in particular, the presence, qualities and quantities of uranium. He had to establish a team of young scientists to work on the project and they would be sworn to secrecy.

The results of their research were to be sent direct to the Scientific Research Institute in Moscow and discussed with no one. The professor himself would also be subjected to constant surveillance to ensure that none of the data was either discussed or released.

Once in Frunze, he quickly became acquainted with his new group of young enthusiastic scientists, who attracted by the nature of the research, were nevertheless unaware of the secret purpose of their work. Amongst them was Tamara. More than the others, she had a special interest in the subject and proved particularly dedicated in her support of the chemist.

Tamara had long dreamt of scrutinizing mineral-rich water and underwater springs. She therefore was well aware that these underground waters had health-improving properties. She therefore became fully absorbed by the project and had never approached any research with such zeal. The fact that their research would progress the development of Kyrgyz science was of specific importance to Tamara and pleased both her and her colleagues. They all believed that their work would be of significant benefit to their country, although they never articulated this.

The work of young scientists involved travel throughout Kyrgyzstan, visiting some of the country's most beautiful regions to collect containers of natural water infused with chemicals from the hot springs.

The chemist Komarov had always believed that his knowledge would be used for the benefit of humanity and never the opposite. He filed reports to Moscow detailing their results which showed that the water from the warm springs contained what they were looking for: Minerals that would be used for the benefit of science and for developing therapeutic treatments. He gave up this information readily, since he knew that it could be used to save many lives.

The laboratory was located in the city centre. Experiments were carried out on the second floor of a grey building that looked no different to any of the city's other Soviet style blocks. The team of young scientists headed by Professor Komarov arrived early in the morning and never left before sunset.

The room where their laboratory was located was small; no larger than twenty square metres. On the south side, a small window let in daylight, and on the right side of the room, stood a built-in, long steel cupboard. In the middle of the room there was a white marble table covered with Soviet-made bottles, flasks and huge canisters. This was where they extracted uranium and other minerals from the underground water that would contribute to the cure of patients with congenital paralysis and many other ailments.

The process was highly developed. It involved the water being evaporated in a controlled manner so that all that remained was a salty residue containing the uranium and other chemicals and minerals. These were then spread over the surface of an iron plate for further analysis and confidentially recorded by Professor Komarov.

The professor was also working concurrently on other research - 'The Erosion and Depletion of Agricultural Soil' - that had no relation with the first project.

Tamara and the other scientists gladly went to Naryn and Issyk-Kul regions to collect huge 20 litre cans of underground water from natural springs, newly formed water wells and fast flowing, mountain rivers.

Although both regions provided very interesting results, the highest concentrations of the best uranium isotopes came from Issyk - Kul.

A special health resort had already been built close to the Ak-Suu gorge whose river runs directly into Issyk-Kul. Also known as 'Warm Springs' it attracted people from all over the former Soviet Union wishing to improve their health, and offered treatments for rheumatism, nervous diseases and varices.

Water from the Ak-Suu gorge was fed into the Centre through a long pipe and the cold water was then mixed with water from the hot radon springs, ready for the procedures. The Centre's main area of specialisation was the complex treatment of cerebral palsy. It was found that the composition of minerals and radon had a strong impact on dead brain cells and helped to restore the neuro-vascular cells. Many patients showed a marked improvement.

The extraordinary natural beauty of the Ak-Suu gorge inspired both Komarov and Tamara as they spent time breathing in the mountain air and walking through the deep gorges filled with the heavy scent of wild flowers. This sense of communing with Nature had a strong impact on their work.

Before coming to Kyrgyzstan, the professor had no idea that his priorities in life would change so dramatically. The people and the wealth of natural beauty of Kyrgyzstan completely changed his views of everything that was happening.

In his diary, he recorded the following:

"I am ready to sacrifice my mind to allow humankind to survive in this bustling world. Being in this place has changed my perspective of the world. I can only direct my knowledge to preserve this natural and pristine beauty. Everything around me is alive and created by God. No one should destroy this glory. No one! Humanity must awaken its consciousness of something much higher and more valuable than the insane world that it is intent on making. No one should dare interfere or destroy the peace of God's wonderful creation."

No one around him was aware of just how much his philosophy on life had changed.

In contrast, their new lifestyle irritated his wife. She felt bored and uncomfortable in Frunze and never gifted at making friends, she showed an unwillingness to socialise with either her husband's staff or her neighbours.

The scientist's wife became increasingly stressed by even the smallest things and often after a quarrel with her husband, cried all night. She pleaded with him to agree to their return to Moscow, where thanks to her husband's contacts, she had enjoyed the high life.

In Frunze, she felt she was simply 'dying away'! She did not understand her husband's enthusiasm and was not going to support his project. Her hysterical attitude towards his work isolated the scientist and increasingly lonely, he immersed himself more fully in his research. It was ruining their marriage. The chemist, in turn, had long ceased to pay any attention to her and did not understand what he was accused of. So, was his whole life now a total lie? Did she no longer love him? Did it really matter?

Each day, she sought comfort from her son by writing to him in red ink. He had studied in Japan and after graduating and against the mother's will, had married a Japanese woman. He now lived there and never visited his parents. His letter home carried a clear statement:

"Dear Mum, I love you both and I am proud of my father, but don't involve me in your relationship. You are both adults and you will sort things out. Your loving son."

These words were the last straw and she vowed that as soon as she could, she would go back to Moscow. Little did she know that she would never again see Moscow! She did not want to understand or support her scientist husband, whose temperament was rapidly changing and who every day, enthusiastically abandoned her for his work.

Time dragged on until one day, the scientist's wife, Lyudmila Afanasyevna, met a tall and startlingly handsome man at the shop. He offered to help carry her groceries home and she was instantly blinded by his attention.

The next day she went to the hairdresser's to have her hair dyed and restyled and thereafter, began to find excuses to wander past and visit the grocery.

With renewed self -confidence, she bought freshly baked curd cake from the local kiosk and decided to invite her neighbour in for tea in an attempt to make new friends. During their conversation, the neighbour asked Lyudmila about the cause of the sobbing which she had heard throughout the night.

On one particular occasion, she had also heard furious shouting through the partition wall and fearing that something was wrong, called the police. They did not find any evidence of physical violence and left soon afterwards. The neighbour later found out that Komarov, the famous scientist, had arrived in Frunze to work on a particularly important task. The sounds that she had subsequently heard coming from next door were angry arguments spurred by his wife's refusal to accept their new circumstances.

They chatted about other things and then Lyudmila Afanasyevna revealed that very soon, she hoped to leave for Moscow and from there, travel to Japan to see her son.

She was about to tell her neighbour about the handsome gentleman she had met at the shop when suddenly, the telephone rang.

Lyudmila Afanasyevna jumped up and answered it immediately.

"Hello, good day. Yes, yes; Stanislav, okay. See you tonight."

She replaced the handset and whilst putting on her shoes, apologized to her neighbour:

"I'm sorry, my dear Veronica, I need to go out. Once again, my husband wants to invite his employees round for drinks and I need to go to the shop."

She put on her cardigan, carefully applied pearl lipstick to her thin lips and left the apartment. When she had gathered all that she needed, she approached the cash register and her heart almost leapt from her chest when she caught sight of the handsome man.

Oh my God, he's here! She tried to compose herself, quickly smoothing her hair whilst trying to look nonchalant.

* * *

"Good day, Lyudmila Afanasyevna." The handsome stranger had suddenly appeared at her side, addressing her in his strange accent.

"Oh, it's you again, kind gentleman. Excuse me!" Caught unawares, she choked on her words and broke into a coughing fit.

He immediately began patting her back.

"Thank you, that'll do. I'm fine now." Lyudmila blushed as she again smoothed her new hairstyle.

"No worries, these things happen." the man reassured her.

"You have not introduced yourself, my dear!" Lyudmila paused and was now flirting and moving like a like a luxuriating cat, aglow from the male attention and oblivious to everything around her.

"I beg your pardon: My name is Boris Ivanov" As he bent to kiss Lyudmila Afanasyevna's trembling hand, Schultz gently stroked her stomach with his spare hand.

As he felt her body tremble at his touch, the spy was more than convinced that this encounter promised a 'fascinating' continuation...

"These women don't need much. In exchange for a bit of flirtation and a hint of romance, she will be ready to sell me anything in the world," Schultz thought with a smirk.

He again proposed to escort her to her house and the presence of this stranger did not escape the notice of her neighbour, who was peeping from behind her curtains.

* * *

Veronica had come to the conclusion that the sobbing during the night was due to loneliness and that it had driven her neighbour to find a young lover.

"She'll play away for a while and then come back to her husband. Any toy is okay if it keeps the baby happy!" She murmured to herself.

Despite these thoughts, she was totally shocked by the antics of this woman from Moscow and as a result, didn't dare tell her husband about Lyudmila's secret meetings with the young man. Dressed to the nines he continued to woo the lonely Lyudmila but there was something suspicious about him and he was forever furtively glancing around as if he were hiding from someone.

It was during this period that the neighbourhood was visited by a construction company in request of the residents' consent for the demolition of buildings to make way for a new urban development.

The professor was out of town on a mission with his staff to explore new sources of radon in the Ak-Suu gorge. He had invited his wife to join them but as usual, she had made a scene and refused because she wanted nothing to do with his work.

Meanwhile, Lyudmila was growing increasingly irritated by her new lover who seemed far more interested in her husband's scholarly research than in her. He spent more time asking her for meticulous details about his work than talking about plans for their future together. She therefore decided to take the initiative and told him that since she had signed over her apartment for demolition and had accepted a large sum in lieu of alternative accommodation, she was now ready to leave this town, and her husband, forever.

She decided to cooperate with her new beau even though she had been surprised when Schultz asked her to steal the keys to Komarov's office.

She took the opportunity to make a copy of the key one night after her husband had fallen asleep, drunk, after one of his house parties. He had just returned from another trip to Lake Issyk-Kul and it annoyed her to see a smile of happiness spread across his face as he slept.

Lyudmila's beau was thus able to proceed with his secret plan to break into the office and steal her husband's work. She did not understand anything that was going on, but excited by the adventure of it all, willingly agreed to be an accomplice in some dizzying intrigue.

He had already booked tickets at the railway station, promising her a long and romantic journey filled with unforgettable and passionate nights.

There was something strange about his behaviour that wildly excited her as he rummaged through her husband's papers. Schultz's eyes burned as he quietly read aloud some of the text and she was amazed when he turned round and spoke to her. Naturally, Lyudmila could not understand why the subject of soil erosion should be of such interest to her handsome adventurer.

Nor did it matter! As far as Lyudmila was concerned, this was where a new phase of her life began. She was now his partner in some intriguing game that promised exciting trips and foreign travel.

Yet, something jarred within her. How could she justify the loss of such important scientific papers composed by her husband? Any doubts however , were fleeting. She could not afford to look backwards. Driven crazy by her new lover's intense and greedy kisses, she felt that everything was circling in space.

The operation was finally completed and at last, it was time for them both to leave for Moscow!

The plan was that she would then accompany him to Germany to complete this mission. Passports and visas would be ready for collection upon their arrival in Moscow. And that would be that! She had to trust him completely. He made her feel really special and as the train started moving, her heart filled with delight with all that was happening.

The August heat raged, only fading at nightfall, as the train trundled through seemingly endless miles of the vast, sparsely populated Kazakh steppe on the first stage of its three-day journey to Moscow. Had it not been for the relentless sound of the train's wheels knocking against the track, it would have been easy to imagine that they had not moved at all.

Three days passed and Lyudmila's new beau, who had promised her nights of unforgettable passion, never touched her. Instead, 'Boris' lent his full concentration to a meticulous examination of the stolen documents...

He reacted abruptly and rudely to her kind and tender touches and every time he pushed her away, Lyudmila felt choked with indignation.

It seemed that he had suddenly become indifferent to her and she felt brutally deceived.

The train conductors eventually announced that the train would be arriving in Moscow within an hour, so passengers should start collecting their belongings and luggage.

"Boris Ivanovich" Lyudmila asked in a cold, formal manner "I've never paid attention to what kind of cigarettes you smoke." She was desperately trying to engage her beau in conversation after three days of silence.

He seemed very nervous about something as he continued writing his notes. Lyudmila was more than concerned by his rough and negative behaviour and she was starting to realize just how stupid she had been. She began to picture the eyes and the face of her husband, who could go to prison for the loss of his uncompleted research project.

"Tea; would anyone like tea? "A plump woman in a railway uniform knocked on the door of their compartment. She was the same attendant who had shown them to their seats back in Frunze.

"No, thank you." Boris tried to respond for both of them as he squeezed past the Conductor to go and stretch his legs by walking along the corridor.

"I'll have tea please" Lyudmila Afanasyevna interjected. Her face revealed how bewildered she felt.

The attendant served her tea and they began chatting as if they had known each other for years. Eventually, the attendant asked:

"Forgive me for such an indiscreet question. How long will you be staying in Moscow?"

Then, without waiting for an answer, she wheeled her trolley with its white cloth cover out of the compartment, closing the door behind her.

At that moment, her companion, the supposed Boris Ivanovich, returned. His face was like thunder.

"What now?" Lyudmila looked at him, ready to burst into tears.

"What do you mean by 'what now?' We have taken the wrong documents!" Her companion began to vent his fury by yelling at her loudly.

Suddenly, the shouting, the train's loud and incessant squeals and the sound of its creaking wheels, became all too much for Lyudmila and screaming, she lunged at him, grabbing at his tie.

In an automatic and violent response, he in turn, clasped his hands around her neck, pushing her backwards so that her head banged against the window. The blow was so hard that for a few seconds, she lost consciousness. As soon as she revived, she instantly started coughing and desperately called for help.

However, Schultz was strong and ruthless. Once again, he grabbed her throat and this time, it ended with the sound of Lyudmila's death rattle as she gasped her final breath.

Distraught, Schultz momentarily fell into a daze but after a while, came to his senses and hurriedly began cleaning up the compartment. He methodically wiped down all surfaces to erase any fingerprints and picked up any cigarette butts that had scattered during the fight.

He was certain that he had not forgotten anything but in the rush, had failed to notice that his unusual tie clip was still clenched in his victim's fist.

Grabbing the briefcase in one hand, he then pulled from beneath the seats, the bag full of money that had belonged to his companion.

As originally planned, Schultz proceeded to the driver's cabin where pressing his gun to the man's head, ordered him to remove his clothes. He then bound the driver's hands and feet and left him lying on the floor. Once disguised in the driver's uniform, Schultz shut the door tightly and disembarked, unnoticed.

By the time Lyudmila's body was discovered, Schultz was already on his way to the airport in the rental car that awaited him outside the station.

He flew direct to Leningrad (St. Petersburg) and from there, took the ferry across the Baltic, before flying to Hungary to meet Rodgers. The plan had been to hand over the documents to the underground organization and then with his financial reward, find Lauren and flee with her to the North Pole.

* * *

Chapter 18

A Murder Investigation, Moscow

Sub-lieutenant Zverev and the criminal detective arrived late from the city morgue. It was a hot August evening. He had now received the results of the forensic examination of the victim.

As they had suspected, the cause of death was a severe brain injury, now confirmed as a brutal hematoma of the right cranial. There were also signs that the victim had been suffocated and there was no trace of any intimate contact. In addition, their evidence included the butt of a foreign Chesterfield cigarette and an unusual tie clip found gripped in the fist of Lyudmila Afanasyevna Komarova.

A call came through from the chief of the railway station.

"Hello, Comrade Sub-lieutenant, please come to the station. We've just found the driver locked in his cabin on the Frunze-Moscow train." The chief of the station was breathing hard and sounded very excited.

"We are on our way" The second lieutenant and his fellow detective jumped into their Lada GAI and rushed at full speed with siren blaring, back to the railway station. The train driver was sitting in the office dressed only in his shorts and shaking with fear.

The driver described how the robber had put a gun to his temple and ordered him to remove his clothes. He had then been told to cover his eyes with his own filthy handkerchief. Fearing for his life, the driver had complied with the stranger's instructions. His mouth was gagged with adhesive tape and once his arms and legs were bound, he was pushed to the floor. However, despite being dazed as he fell and everything happening so fast, the driver had managed to catch a glimpse of the man through a gap in his blindfold. He also saw two briefcases and remembered that one was made from high quality leather.

"What else did you see?" The detective asked, screwing up his sharp eyes, whilst automatically taking notes and making sketches of the two briefcases.

"There's a lot more to this than just the murder!" The detective muttered to himself, deep in thought. He got up and started to pace around the room.

"Is there anything to suggest that the strangled victim was somehow involved in abduction or had interfered with any criminal organization?" He expressed his thoughts aloud and looked intently at sub-lieutenant Zverev.

"Let's assume that this is the case. There were two briefcases, probably containing documents or money. What else could be deemed more valuable than classified or some form of secret documents or stolen money? Have there been reports of any bank robberies?" As Zverev finished his second cup of strong tea, his mind was racing and he was suddenly struck by the most ridiculous idea – was Komarov, the eminent scientist and husband of the victim, the head of some terrible gang responsible for this incident? Could it be that this case might develop into something of national importance? "We need to find out how the scientist is involved!" Loosening his collar and scratching his head, Zverev called the airport and booked a seat on the first available flight to Frunze.

It would be easier to conduct his investigation on site and it was imperative that he questioned Komarov as soon as possible.

Before leaving, they had to produce an image of the man described by the train driver. Dressing the poor driver in the only clothes available – an old cleaner's coat – they quickly escorted him to the offices of the local KGB where a specialist drew a portrait of the only suspect known to them so far. The sketch was then circulated to airports and railway stations in Moscow and Leningrad as well as cities with international transport connections.

Neither the detective nor sub-lieutenant Zverev managed to sleep that night.

The next morning, Zverev boarded a flight to Frunze where he would inform the scientist of his wife's murder and then take him into custody for questioning. He had to establish the reason why she had fled Kyrgyzstan with the man alleged to be her lover.

The young police officer felt like he had wound up in an action-packed thriller and was so exhausted that he slept through the entire flight to Frunze.

* * *

Tamara and her staff had just returned from a trip, and were now standing with 20-litre cans of underground spring water in front of the high security building.

Her heart skipped a beat when she saw that police had surrounded their laboratory. They were now in the process of calling in everyone for questioning, one by one.

In Karakol Prejevalsk at the Eastern end of Lake Issyk-Kul a call came through from the department of the State Security Committee to the local chief of the Department of Internal Affairs with instructions for Komarov's arrest. Without a word of explanation, the local chief tracked down Komarov at the town's main hotel where he was handcuffed and taken by armed guard to Frunze, Kyrgyzstan's capital city.

The scientist did not understand the reason for his arrest and the police officer handcuffed to him and who regarded him rather obliquely, told him nothing throughout the journey. On arrival, he was taken into custody and accused of the contracted murder of his wife Lyudmila Afanasyevna. He was told that he would remain a prime suspect until the investigation had been completed.

Komarov was so traumatised by this totally unexpected turn of affairs that he fainted several times during his interrogation.

It was later discovered that his briefcase had been stolen from his office but the key to his safe was still where he had left it, hidden beneath a carpet under a chair in his office.

The missing documents related to his work for the Moscow laboratory and the reason for his move to Kyrgyzstan. This scientific research was something he had dreamt of from a young age and was his personal brainchild. It was allegedly known only to Moscow, Komarov and his team of scientists.

He could not comprehend why his wife and her new beau would have been so interested in this unfinished scientific work. Perhaps one of his rivals had set them up?

Komarov had no particular enemies. Perhaps a few of his scientific colleagues were envious of his research success but he could not think of anyone that would have gone to such drastic measures.

As far as the investigation was concerned, everything currently pointed to Komarov, leading to a potential charge of treason for the sale of his highly specialised, scientific research.

Confronted with news of the betrayal, the murder of his wife and then the loss of years' of research, Komarov had never felt so weak and bewildered. He was shocked to the core by all that he had lost.

The following day his colleagues from Moscow interceded and asked that he was cleared of any suspicion of treason. An unidentified source had returned his research papers to the Research Institute of the USSR Academy of Sciences.

Meanwhile, his neighbour Veronica, had been able to provide a description of Lyudmila's lover, whom she had frequently seen entering and leaving their apartment. Her description matched almost perfectly, the sketch based on the description provided by the driver of the Frunze- Moscow train.

According to the neighbour, Lyudmila had become completely besotted by this handsome man and longed to return to Moscow with him, so that together, they could embrace the more exciting, social lifestyle that she had previously enjoyed. Lyudmila had spoken often about the marvellous parties in Moscow and Veronica, offering a sympathetic ear, had understood how much she missed the company of the other scientists' wives.

Lyudmila had lived in Moscow's city centre in a special quarter, which had its own security and its own range of privileges. However, Komarov, her husband had been less enamoured of Moscow's city life and therefore welcomed his appointment to lead on a special research project in Kyrgyzstan. This was the culmination of years of hard endeavour and numerous proposals to the Scientific Council of the Academy of Sciences in Moscow. Komarov felt like his soul had at last taken flight. He would now have the freedom to advance his research in the fresh air of a natural environment. He had long dreamt of escaping the city and the feeling of being sucked into its quagmire of monotonous routine and idle chatter.

Chapter 19

Professor Komarov

Komarov had never felt it necessary to join the Communist Party.

In the past, Stalin had done everything in his power to exclude scholars from politics, through fear of their general anti-government attitude. This explained the generous provision of facilities and salaries for scientists and researchers in other fields.

Later on, rules changed, and all scientists were obliged to join the Party so that their work could be carefully monitored. The default behaviour of the Political Bureau of the Party workers, which hung in the air like an axe, sometimes drove Komarov to distraction. There were many reasons for this. Science had become both lucrative and dangerous, which sharpened the focus on what was going on within the scientific community. The stakes were high and this was reflected in hot 'debates' within genetics, applied physics and many other scientific fields. The rising cries of the threat of a 'cold war' between the socialist countries and the West, particularly America, inspired all scientists to conduct very careful work. Countries participating in the arms race became ever more committed to chasing each other's scientific achievements.

The chemist understood the advantages and disadvantages of the different systems and this knowledge informed his awareness of the inherent dangers. He knew that his secret research was being carefully monitored and protected and that there would always be someone wanting to steal it.

"I am a scientist to my finger-tips. I am a patriot of my people! We scientists, have nothing to do with politics. We do not want to be party leaders. What science needs is a broader arena."

Komarov often thought about such things but didn't dare keep a diary or record his views. There was always a 'colleague' at his side to whom Komarov disclosed nothing of his thoughts or views before his daily retreat behind the locked door of his lab. Only then, with the window open wide to let in the cool fresh air, could he relax.

As an influential scholar, he often thought of his father. When Komarov was still a young boy, his father had suffered the terrible consequences of an anonymous campaign against him to the KGB and he was deported by Stalin to Siberia. He was an outstanding engineer, talented and full of energy, who had served his country day and night, often cold and hungry, throughout the Second World War.

However, an anonymous letter accused him of being a spy for the American intelligence. It was enough to initiate a case against him, despite any evidence or clarification of circumstances, and he was mercilessly condemned and exiled to Siberia. In his letters home, he asked just one thing of his wife: to go to his friend in Leningrad. This friend had the power to offer protection to their son and daughter and provide them with an education.

Komarov had been very young at the time but often recalled with a shiver that penetrated his whole being, the night his family was forced to leave Moscow. His father had insisted in his letters to his mother that she disown him and therefore, well aware of the consequences of her husband's conviction, she changed the family's surname so that their children would be free to continue their education. His older sister followed in her father's footsteps and studied to be an engineer. Komarov graduated from high school with honours and later excelled at university. After completing graduate school, he returned to the Department of Biology and Chemistry, where still young, he defended his first scientific paper.

Then came a breakthrough and he was able to visit Siberia. Komarov laid flowers on the mass grave of the prisoners who had perished, and wept long and hard beside the stone that he had engraved in honour of his father.

After this trip, his goal was clear! He was first and foremost a scientist: a chemist who would remain patriotic to his country.

He would however, always tread carefully to avoid the same fate as his father.

When his sister graduated from college, she married a fellow engineer. They both joined Komsomol and were sent to work in Cuba. They wrote no letters, as they were ever wary of attracting even the slightest attention.

Komarov's background and work made him constantly suspicious and he could sometimes feel alarmed by even the sudden rustle of paper or the sound of a light wind. At times, he felt that even his thoughts were overheard by everyone around him. He knew that his paranoia sometimes made him look like an idiot, especially when walking alone, he often muttered to himself.

All he wanted was a laboratory in which he could work, far from the chaos of everyday life. His key objective was to contribute to the development of science and to encourage the growth of the next generation of scientists. He would direct all his knowledge and abilities solely towards the salvation of humanity!

Komarov was ready to dedicate his life to the study of the properties of water, both on the land and underground.

Whatever life threw at him, he knew he would always love his country, but he was also aware that the systems which operated within this powerful nation had their own unique dangers and disadvantages.

This was illustrated by a case involving one of his employees. A young and enthusiastic man, who had only been recently appointed, sent a small card to his girlfriend. At the end, he added a joke: "To Lenin and his comrades - a red flag for each of their hands."

The card was returned to him and a Komsomol meeting was arranged directly in front of the small narrow room usually occupied by the concierge. She had been asked to vacate the room for a very important event. The young scientist's behaviour had greatly disturbed certain members of Komsomol as well as party members and his colleagues in the laboratory, and the meeting turned into a serious interrogation.   At the entrance to the office, the young comrade stood rooted to the spot, guiltily staring at the floor. He avoided looking at the portrait of Lenin hanging on the wall and the eyes of the proletariat leader, which seemed to accuse him from within the gilt frame.

"What gave you the right to treat the leader of our revolution with such disrespect?" barked a bearded fellow with glasses, well known for his loud rants at party meetings.

"You seem to have forgotten that all communist scientists should, and must, be grateful to Comrade Stalin, who in 1946 raised your salaries! We should bow down and remember the privileges that he bestowed upon scientists so that they could make a decent living through their work in the name of our leaders and for the benefit of the proletariat! Scientists owe them their careers and the very air they breathe! Without them, all of you would have been sent to plough the fields and been given sickles to harvest the grain by hand. Would you have preferred the noble profession of the agricultural workforce and farmers which provided us with food throughout the forties, 50's and 60's?"

"Dear comrades! In my note, I praised Lenin, our leader." The young man nervously stammered as if he had committed a terrible crime.

His comrades had a long discussion and then condemned his action. He was expelled from Komsomol and worse, it was decided to make public, the reason for his dismissal. This meant that he would be unable to secure another job in his field and from that moment on, his options for employment were reduced to menial labouring work such as that of a janitor or dustman.

His papers now recorded that he had been 'fired for the mockery of Lenin, leader of proletariat.' The doors to scientific research were now closed to him. No one wanted to hire him and risk bringing trouble to their organisations.

The young scientist, who had fallen into a full depression, was now seen riding around Moscow on his bicycle, looking for a job with which to support himself.

Komarov frequently tried to help this young man who had inadvertently kissed goodbye to opportunities offered by any scientific institution. His helplessness tore him apart: what a foolish way to have his life, destiny and future ruined. How could this young man's employers have acted in such a blind and heartless manner!

Now, more importantly, what could Komarov do for him?

The situation reminded him keenly of the past, when a simple anonymous letter against his father had robbed him of everything in life, including his name.

Checks on personal letters or parcels were the norm but because Komarov believed that his former employee had been an innocent victim of such surveillance, he was determined to help him as much as possible.

This form of mental pressure exerted by those who called themselves the 'people's commissars' continues to this day but it was under Stalin, that the existence of this punitive force began to be practised in the form of a special cult. Its members were often regarded as 'cold shadows'. In the workplace, their identities were invisible and any discussions in public areas never extended beyond issues concerning the ordinary administration of offices or staff. The trails of these seemingly innocuous and usually unsuccessful government employees and managers of small businesses could be detected in every fuggy corridor, as they tirelessly watched over more successful employees and young, promising scientists.

Value was placed on those who held lowly diplomas and they were appointed to high positions, regardless of their lack of experience. This is turn, led to a rapid degradation of society which had a devastating effect on the increasingly undermined working class amongst whom, alcoholism now soared. The recognition that those holding mediocre diplomas were more easily manipulated, with regard to the implementation of ideological propaganda, also undermined the prestige previously afforded to academics and specialists, from teachers and engineers to high level scientists.

The degradation of education has disastrous results eventually leading to poorer and poorer performance in the economy.

There are always two sides to every coin.

On one side, there are people who spend their lives intent on destroying the lives of others in the name of patriotism. They declare themselves true communists. On the other, there are those who are fervently challenged by the cell of 'uncouth fools' that undermines the credibility of real scientists and real patriots.

Komarov believed the co-existence of these different layers to be universal and ageless, affecting human societies worldwide and throughout history, to varying degrees.

As time passed, he became increasingly concerned for the welfare of his former, young employee and regularly met him in the park to give him money saved from his own salary so that he wouldn't die of hunger and depression.

One day, the young man did not appear. Komarov immediately began to search for him, to no avail. Terrible thoughts flooded through his mind: had he committed suicide? Entering the young man's apartment, he found a watch and a note to his girlfriend:

"I don't blame you for any part in this. We are all faithful to Lenin. I remain in my heart and soul, a true member of Komsomol. Your loving friend."

In the apartment, he also found old clothes and a filthy overall, perhaps from the period when the frustrated scientist worked in a waste-processing shop in Moscow.

A bookshelf, which was packed with the works of Mayakovsky, confirmed that a person living in the apartment was an admirer of the Soviet poet.

One of the books he had been reading lay open on his desk. Its pages fluttered gently in a light draft wafting from the window which opened out to a small balcony. Surveying the scene, Komarov was filled with intense feelings of emptiness and sadness.

This case took its toll on the chemist and within a couple of months, he had lost a lot of weight and aged considerably. When all efforts to find the body of the man who had suddenly disappeared failed, Komarov submitted a special application to the local prosecutor's office with a picture and details of the missing man. The young scientist was an orphan and it was up to Komarov alone, to care for him like a father.

He lived in hope that one day, he would be found.

Again, he reminded himself "One cannot be too careful."

The laboratory staff along with those who called themselves 'commissars' continued their lives as usual. They congratulated themselves on the successful removal of the non-Communist from their group. The fact that they had destroyed the promising future of a very intelligent young scientist was of no concern. They were too deeply embedded in a quietly rotting system fuelled by blasphemy and corruption to see beyond their noses. After work and over the weekends, they gathered in pubs, as heavy drinking was an inherent part of the ugly lifestyle of a generation for which communism had achieved cult status. City police systematically gathered up the drunks sprawled throughout the city and sent them to one of the many rehabilitation centres where they were enrolled in community service.

This phenomenon frightened the scientist. He worried that such degradation would not lead to anything good in the future.

Given all that had happened, Komarov was elated when he heard that the Research Institute Board had accepted his application to work in Kyrgyzstan.

Leaving Moscow would set him free to finally focus on long harboured projects but he was also obliged to concentrate on a secret project that had been entrusted to him.

Shortly after his arrival in Frunze, Komarov received a postcard, unsigned and with no return address. His heart started pounding. He spent a while looking with pleasure at the image on the front of a beautiful, vast forest in Trans Baikal. He felt his spirits rise and his eyes shone with happiness. He alone, understood the value of the unsigned postcard. It was a sign that his former young colleague was alive!

Anything was possible!

The scientist was elated and hummed happily as he set off for work.

* * *

In 1944, the German militia began to employ missile technology and by the end of the Second World War, these highly effective weapons were coveted by every country of the conquering allies.

To end the Second World War in 1945 and in response to Japan's declaration that it would never cease military operations, the USA dropped two atomic bombs on the two major Japanese cities: Hiroshima and Nagasaki. This set the course of world geopolitics for the the next half century.

In 1952 Britain detonated its first nuclear bomb.

When Khrushchev led the USSR from 1950 to 1960, competition for the production of military weaponry between the US and the Soviet Union accelerated.

In 1961 the Cold War- a war of spies - entered its most serious phase following the construction of the Berlin Wall as part of the Iron Curtain. "M.A.D." - Mutually Assured Destruction where both sides would effectively launch their atomic missiles and guarantee total destruction of the civilised world - was the main restraint of the atomic arms race.

In 1961 - Kennedy announced America's plans to lead the space race and be the first country to put a man on the moon.

1969 – American Neil Armstrong took his first steps on the moon; a significant event which marked the end of the space race.

Later, Russia's hero cosmonaut Grechko described the space race as 'one of the greatest Olympic competitions of mankind.'

* * *

Chapter 20

Frunze, Kyrgyzstan

The interrogations headed by sub-lieutenant Zverev opened up far more lines of inquiry and investigations than he had envisaged.

All of Komarov's secret documents were in place in the scientist's office, with the exception of one uncompleted project. It had been recently stolen and there seemed no logical reason for its theft to be attributed to the chemist's wife or her new lover.

A call then came through from his colleagues in Moscow, advising him that all accusations against Komarov for murder or treason had been cleared. Zverev later received a parcel, which he handed over to the Professor.

Whilst in Moscow, the sub-lieutenant had been made aware of the secretive nature of the scientist's research and was frankly daunted by the potential complexity of the case, which would further stretch his capabilities. Due to his lack of experience, he realized that he would need to focus his full attention on identifying the thread, which linked the clues and motives behind this complicated case which now extended far beyond murder.

He felt as though he were playing a character in an intriguing detective novel and out of his depth, could not envisage a simple solution, for him at least.

Exhausted after such a challenging day, he returned to Komarov's office and locking the door, began a close examination of the scientist's correspondence with both the Academic Council and Department of State Security.

The next morning, Komarov was released on bail. His son, Pavel, after being alerted of the situation by friends, had immediately taken the first flight from Japan to Moscow, and from there, to Frunze.

He had now arrived at the airport in Frunze where Zvervev met him. As they stood on the concourse of the newly constructed marble building, the sub-lieutenant updated him on the background and progress of the complicated case involving Pavel's father.

Pavel only relaxed when he saw that his father was alive and well, although proof of his innocence was still required to clear him of any further accusation. Pavel therefore decided to return to Moscow to bury his mother.

Still under house arrest, Komarov was unable to join him but in any case, he was in no fit state to fly. The impact of the events of the past few days had left him confused and frightened, affecting both his physical and mental health.

Once in Moscow, Pavel identified the body of his mother, Lyudmila Afanasyevna, and buried her in the city's cemetery, close to her family. It proved a prolonged and stressful experience and he was glad that his wife flew in from Japan to support him.

"Sleep well, you're at home now." Pavel cried loudly from grief and frustration. He could not understand how on earth his mother had managed to get involved in this terrible saga.

Before leaving Moscow, he made a few calls to his friends, asking them to carry out a thorough investigation and restore the good name of his father, in whose innocence he had no doubt. He was returning to Japan with a heavy heart. The events surrounding his father would affect him too.

"My son, everything will be fine. This mess will linger on for a long time. If I lose my job, it would mean losing everything. You cannot do anything here. Do not ruin your life for my sake. You must stay away from all this chaos." insisted Professor Komarov in a letter to Pavel.

He knew however, that whatever the outcome, from this day on he would remain under constant surveillance and would never again be left alone.

Komarov's head was spinning. He kept thinking about the young scientist whom he had been unable to defend, and could not allow his own son to suffer because of this situation, over which Komarov had no control.

It was only the unsigned card which stopped him from falling into an even deeper depression.

Pavel and his Japanese wife had left in the knowledge that they would never again be able to re-enter the country. The case had acquired catastrophic consequences which had destroyed the very foundations of the scientist's life and family.

All of Komarov's employees and former colleagues were repeatedly called to the KGB office where the Soviet scientists were questioned. Their fingerprints were taken and there was a thorough inspection of all their research work.

No one was prepared for the ensuing chaos and every employee felt nervous as they rushed to work each morning.

The knowledge that their laboratory and their conversations were now under surveillance, finally drove some employees to a nervous breakdown and many left their jobs voluntarily. Nobody knew what had happened, and no one explained the reasons for this mess.

It was hard for them to focus on their research especially since all scientific experiments had been suspended.

At the same time, parallel restrictions were imposed on other branches of the Kyrgyz SRR Academy of Sciences, including the Institutes of Inorganic Chemistry, Physics, Mathematics, Automation, Biology and Geology. The Scientific Research Institutes had now acquired a special status within the ranks of the Intelligence Services, which related to all of the Research Institutes of the Kyrgyz SSR.

The Institute of Inorganic Chemistry, where Komarov and Tamara worked, was now completely immured by law enforcement agencies, which day and night, kept watch over their building and their activities.

* * *

Chapter 21

Time Moves On

Komarov, the esteemed academic, spent a long period in a psychiatric clinic. He frequently ran away and then returned, always apologizing to the staff. Whenever he grew over excited, he was calmed with strong sedatives and in Tamara's eyes, this was a blessing. Whilst suspended in this state, he remembered nothing and was unaware of what had become of his laboratory.

Their joint work on evaporated water could not progress because of the necessity of further laboratory tests. Its future was unknown.

Tamara recognized that her best years had been invested in this lost research and she had yet to defend her doctoral thesis. But her career as a scientist seemed settled. Assisted by Alexei, she regularly travelled to Moscow, London, Brussels and other cities to deliver lectures and meet other scientists. She loved teaching.

For a while they were able to work together at the same university but in 1993 Alexei moved to Moscow with his parents and from there, immigrated to Israel.

At that time, the country was going through difficult times and many Jews and Germans who had lived for long periods in the former Soviet Union, decided to leave.

* * *

Tamara watched everything as it unfolded and saw how it affected people's lives. From time to time, she hugged her mother and tried to offer assurance by telling her "Don't worry, everything will be alright."

The city was changing rapidly. It was particularly difficult to witness the effects on the elderly. Reduced to sitting on the streets at the entrances of buildings, many now spent their days trying to sell bits and pieces of old furniture and other artefacts from their homes.

All fifteen Soviet Republics had peacefully gained their independence almost overnight and in Kyrgyzstan, a short contest was held for the best national emblem and national flag.

Disputes arose between former Communists. Some handed over their Party tickets, completely disillusioned, whilst others remained true to the cause. The days of a single ideology were over.

What had become of the 'bright future', awaited by citizens for over seventy years?

The shelves in the stores lay empty for months and supplies of food from foreign countries were not expected in the near future. The systems which operated from Moscow, into which all fifteen republics had contributed food for even distribution, were looted and dissolved. Factories were closed, one after the other, or privatized. Thousands of people became unemployed.

Construction sites were abandoned, leaving huge beams protruding from unfinished walls. Older sites or houses, only recently signed off by the city authorities for demolition, awaited their fate.

Chaos reigned.

* * *

Chapter 22

Bishkek (formerly Frunze), Kyrgyzstan, 2014

Tamara had been troubled by disturbing thoughts for a long time. She was particularly worried about the state of Professor Komarov and feedback from his doctors offered small comfort. She had become aware of bizarre developments in his behaviour, especially the disappearances and re-appearances at the hospital, and realized that he had embarked on some sort of game. After many years of working together, Tamara knew her mentor well.

She had once tried to find him on her way home, in the place where she had first seen him, but he was not there.

Tamara could not accept what had happened to this unique man. What had been the link between his dead wife and his research? The question swirled around in her head. It seemed like a nightmare.

Tamara decided to share her concerns and suspicions about the sudden appearance and disappearance of the professor with Alexei. Over the phone, they discussed at length, the consequences which a series of inconclusive events had had on his life and resolved to organize their own investigation.

In spite of Alexei's entreaties for her to do nothing until he arrived in Bishkek, Tamara decided to take the perilous risk of beginning her own search for the scientist.

* * *

Spring had finally arrived after a long, hard winter.

Birdsong mingled in a sweet symphony, as Tamara opened her small window to inhale the spring air.

She thought about what she could wear as a disguise for her mission and decided upon her mother's old grey coat and her grandmother's glasses. She had found both of these amongst old clothes at her parents' cottage, when she had come to dig over the garden and ventilate the house after winter. Each spring, the whole family descended on the country house to put everything in order. Her mother and father preferred to spend spring and summer in the countryside's fresh air, far away from the bustle and stuffiness of the city.

A green scarf, gifted by Alexei, would complete her outfit.

"My God, how weird I'll look!" exclaimed Tamara, laughing at her choice of outfit for the start of her mission.

"Hmm… it smells like there's a touch of frost in the air." She muttered, twitching her nose as she moved outside.

Spring had come early but warnings about storms and sudden cold snaps were normal in this beautiful mountainous country at this time of year.

The garden which had begun to bloom, warmed by yesterday's sunshine, had been nipped by frost overnight and her heart sank at the sight. The rigors of the continental climate could be cruel and like people, the plants and trees sometimes had to struggle hard to survive.

Gathering up the remainder of last year's foliage, she managed to start a fire. Smoke began to spread lazily over the garden.

Leaning on her rake, she sighed heavily; "let's hope this year brings a good crop of apricots and cherries, so that we we'll have enough to sell and still keep a good amount for ourselves."

* * *

The next evening, dressed in her disguise, Tamara took the bus for a couple of stops up to the hospital. She hid herself in the farthest corner of a long corridor where she could keep an eye on visitors coming and going.

When she last visited the professor, she had met a young nurse in a green robe and could now see the same nurse standing at her desk. The desk was a little further down the corridor than the room that Tamara was interested in.

The clock on the wall showed nine o'clock.

Although tired from waiting, she began to feel nervous.

Perhaps today's mission wouldn't be possible after all? She felt doubtful but was desperate to believe in the success of her plan.

Well, it's clear that if I'm to make a good spy, I can't afford to be hesitant!

Chiding herself and removing her headscarf, Tamara walked boldly down the corridor.

She had already got half-way, when suddenly, the door to the room which she had been watching, opened and none other than the professor, stuck his head out before quietly retreating inside.

Tamara paused: This was the moment she had been waiting for! She hastily replaced her scarf.

The nurse, who was busily writing up her notes, looked up when she saw an old woman appear from nowhere.

Tamara had to do something! Gathering her thoughts, she adopted the voice of an elderly woman and enquired after the health of Komarov.

"Komarov? Komarov: You mean Professor Komarov? Oh ... I'm sorry, but may I ask who's asking after him?" Replied the young nurse, taken by surprise. No one ever asked after this patient or came to visit him.

"Uh, excuse me, what?" Tamara gently shook her head and adjusted her glasses.

The nurse repeated the question slowly.

"Me? A-ah, I am a concierge. I know ... I know." she feigned a bout of nervous coughing.

"Would you like some water?" The nurse asked sympathetically, as she guided Tamara to the nearest bench.

"Oh-oh, yes please." The 'old lady' coughed even harder.

The nurse dashed off, empty glass in hand, to the end of the corridor where Tamara had previously been hiding and was irritated to discover that the old woman had disappeared by the time she got back. Clicking her tongue, the nurse shrugged and resumed her work, periodically glancing around her. Feeling slightly unnerved, she almost leapt from her chair when her phone rang.

"Hello, this is the psychiatric ward's duty nurse speaking. Can you hear me? Hello ... Hello ... Hello?" There was a short beep and the unknown caller hung up.

Once again, she looked down the corridor, trying to stave off frightening thoughts, and then returned to her computer.

Meanwhile, Tamara had slipped into the room next to Komarov's. She replaced her mobile phone in the pocket of her mother's old grey coat.

It worked! Filled with a childish glee, Tamara resisted the urge to clap her hands as she peeped through a crack in the door. Her heart was pounding.

She recovered her breath and slowly shifted her gaze so that she could better survey the room. It was completely empty.

She leant against the wall, hugging her heavy bag and feeling utterly exhausted and completely overstrung. The ground seemed to crumble beneath her feet and she gently slipped to the floor. Here she remained, her mind blank, staring out of the window.

She was engulfed in a silent darkness, broken only by the faint glow of a streetlight outside the window.

I have to get out of here before the main entrance is locked: But how? She began to consider her options. Should she wait until the nurse left her desk and make a run for it?

Tamara could not afford for her appearance to be registered and later recalled by anyone. She needed leeway to come and go in order to find out what was going on with the professor and had no idea how long that might take.

Suddenly, someone crept past the window and approached the window of the next room. Once again her granny's glasses proved more than useful. She could clearly see a tall, slender young man with slightly curly long hair. He was neither Komarov's son, nor any of the professor's associates.

Tamara silently moved to the window, stretched up, and gently opened it. Cool air rushed into the room, accompanied by the voice of the stranger who was earnestly whispering:

"Stanislav Petrovich ... Professor ... Are you ready?"

The man then deftly removed the metal grill from the window and she heard puffing sounds as the professor climbed out.

The young man refitted the grill to the window, checked that their path was clear and then he and the professor made for the gate.

Tamara could barely resist the urge to cry out: "Help! Wait! I'll come with you!"

She tried to lift the grill form the window in her room but it was securely fixed and would not budge.

She could not afford to lose them! Tamara opened her door and quickly scanned the corridor. Two patients were standing alongside each other against the wall but the nurse had gone.

Tamara grabbed her heavy bag and rushed to the room from which the professor and his unknown companion had just escaped.

The window had been closed and the grill replaced. She desperately started looking for a gap through which she could push her hand to unscrew the bolts, cursing herself for not calling out to them.

Eventually, she managed to lift the grill and pushing it so that it swung open, Tamara hastily climbed through the window and quietly began her decent. It was quite a drop and she gasped as she hit the ground below.

She sped across the carpark towards the gate but the men were nowhere to be seen. When she passed the guard, she nodded to him out of habit, wishing him goodnight.

* * *

Sighing heavily she hailed a taxi and returned home late.

Noticing her very strange attire, her elderly mother began to question her as soon as she walked in the door. Tamara knew that she would be interrogated but managed to stall her:

Alright, Mum. I will tell you everything. Just wait a minute."

She took off the old grey coat and after washing her face, poured herself a brandy. Tamara then explained to her mother how she had tried to reach a former colleague, who was now a patient in the psychiatric clinic.

The old woman could not believe her ears and as Tamara talked, she nervously clutched at the collar of her blouse.

She eyed her daughter suspiciously whilst trying to fathom her behaviour and longed to find out more. But it was now well after midnight so she turned out the lights and they both retired to bed.

Alone in her room, she set the alarm to wake Tamara in time for work but could not help but sigh, "One of these days, my daughter will drive me crazy".

Tamara could not get to sleep. Her head was awash with questions about all that she had witnessed.

"Who was that young man? Had he come to help the chemist? I've never seen him before!"

She continued talking to herself whilst mentally revisiting the scene in the hospital.

Finally, at daybreak, she got up and wrote an email to Alexei with an update of what had happened and was encouraged by his immediate response:

"Dear Tamara, This is great news! Wait for my arrival! Yours, Alexei."

However, Tamara had already worked out her own plan!

Buildings constructed during the Soviet era had deep cellars. Perhaps she would find her answers in the cellars of the old lab? People often retreated to the cellars when soldiers descended upon the city and during air raids. They had been told that the walls and ceilings had been built to withstand the impact of atomic bombs but the scientists knew that in such an event, the only survivors were likely to be rats and cockroaches.

Tamara had become completely engrossed in her mission and it felt special to be part of something so intriguing.

She was now eager to visit the site of their old lab. Half of the building had been closed up and none of labs were now in operation. Most of the young scientists had long ago moved abroad to continue their academic studies. The only facility that remained open belonged to a local academic council, which had managed to survive without support from the State.

After listening to the morning news, Tamara made quick preparations and went out. The sun warmed the streets that were already choked with dust and fumes from the heavy traffic. Impatient, Tamara took a taxi rather than wait for a bus and felt quite emotional at the prospect of visiting her old lab in the city centre.

She slowly approached the front door and was surprised to find it open and unpatrolled by guards. She mechanically went downstairs to the basement where she found another heavy door.

Quietly pulling the handle, she entered a long corridor. She felt like she had entered some sort of creepy maze and was fearful of the ghostly figures that she imagined lurking within its silent emptiness.

Nevertheless, she could not afford to let her imagination wander. She was here for a purpose: to focus on answers to the unresolved circumstances which had led to her professor's breakdown.

Tamara began her search despite not knowing what she was looking for. The high ceilings made the space cavernous but her confidence grew when she flicked the light switch and a lamp came on, albeit dim. As she gingerly proceeded along the long corridor, she suddenly noticed some figures in the distance and for a few seconds she froze. Then pulling herself together, cried out:

"Stanislav Petrovich! Comrade Komarov!"

As her voice echoed throughout the vast space, two figures started walking towards her. They halted close by and then one of them replied:

Who are you and what do you want?

Tamara was overcome with emotion and summoning her courage, shouted:

"Stanislav Petrovich! It's me; Tamara!"

The two figures rushed forward and Tamara burst into tears of joy and relief when her former colleague grabbed her in a warm embrace.

"Oh, my God! I can`t believe it!"

She hugged the white-haired scientist close, delighted that he appeared healthy and in fine spirits.

"Tamara, is it really you? "

The scientist was clearly astonished to see her there.

"What are you doing here? This is supposed to be a secret location, known only to me and my assistant!"

"You're here ... and you're in white coats ... your assistant?" She stammered, unable to voice her thoughts quickly enough.

"Come with us" beckoned Komarov "but you must promise me that you will not say a word to anyone. Not even your family."

Komarov and his assistant then guided Tamara through a long corridor and turning a corner, opened a heavy iron door to reveal a spacious lab.

Tamara looked in awe at the large, brightly lit lab, well equipped with modern appliances. Its warm atmosphere and light smells of chemicals felt so familiar to her that once again, Tamara was reduced to tears.

"What on earth is this?" exclaimed Tamara. It looked exactly the same as the lab where they had all worked together, many years ago. She quickly pulled out her handkerchief and mirror, to wipe away the mascara that had been smeared by her tears, and waited for the professor to respond.

"Come to my office and I will explain everything. But first of all, let me introduce you to my assistant, Igor Vasilyevich. He is a scientist with whom I worked in Moscow during the early years. He left the city without telling me where he had gone but later on, I received a strange, unsigned postcard with no return address and deep in my heart, I knew that one day, he would find me.

Since then, strict measures have been in place to prevent either of us continuing scientific research but we were determined to work together on a subject for which we share a passion. Now I think I should make us a cup of strong tea!"

As her professor started taking cups from a cupboard, he continued, "I was once approached by a very pleasant woman named Lauren, who warned me of plans by an organization to procure important documents. These related to highly sensitive research that I had been secretly working on in tandem to my soil erosion project and had attracted the interest of foreign spies. Clandestine enemies of the Cold War were also involved. They were already arranging, with assistance from my late wife, to steal the papers that I had yet to complete. There was nothing I could do. I had to cooperate with her, in order to stay alive. We had to make compromises and allow them to steal the key to my office, which my wife had taken from my pocket, whilst I pretended to be drunk. In the aftermath, I was instructed to plead ignorance about the whole state of affairs and was warned that I would be arrested. Lauren assured me that the stolen papers would be returned to me later and my reputation would be untarnished. If I had been found guilty of being an accomplice in that nightmarish operation, I would have been punished for treason of the State!"

"What of your late wife? Why were you unable to warn her?" asked Tamara, sipping her tea.

"My wife was to have 'disappeared', but something went badly wrong and she was caught in a fatal situation. I could not do anything to help her. Everything happened so very quickly. The spy who killed her adopted a false identity and managed to escape from the train. He has never been detained and appears to have gone into hiding. The briefcase containing my stolen documents had been intercepted by the Conductor. She had replaced it with another after she became deeply suspicious of the spy who had been with my wife. The original documents were returned to me safely by sub-lieutenant Zverev who was involved in the investigation of this complicated operation. All was going to plan and the operation would have been a success, had it not been for an unexpected turn of events. No one could have anticipated that the spy would kill the key witness. My wife would hopefully have run away as soon as they got off the train. Instead, she was murdered. I will never forgive myself for not being able to save her."

Suddenly overcome with remorse, Komarov began to weep.

"Come, my dear: May her soul rest in peace. You must not blame yourself. It was an accident. You could not have helped her. She betrayed you." Tamara approached the scientist, trying to comfort him.

Wiping his tears with a handkerchief, Komarov took a deep breath and continued his extraordinary story.

"Unable to forgive myself, I ceased to believe that I would ever be able to stand again on my own two feet. By the time Igor found me, I had lost all hope. When he heard from mutual friends that I was in a psychiatric clinic at a health resort, he decided to find me and propose that we work together. The first time he visited me, he did not reveal that he had managed to equip and make operational, the lab in this abandoned basement. I was still very ill but luckily, a young doctor named Alfia Yurievna had just come to practice in the hospital. A gifted physician with near magical skills, she put me back on my feet. To this day, she continues to save the lives of numerous patients, especially children, and I am deeply indebted to her. As soon as I had fully recovered, I joined Igor to continue working in secret, on my uncompleted research project. It was only the continuation of my work that saved me. This lab has now been operational for a number of years. I also have the full support of my son. At the beginning, he managed to sneak back into the country from Japan, to ensure that everything was in place and since then, has funded this little lab. We continue to contribute to the Academic Council's scientific policies concerning the environment although the prolonged neglect of such issues by local government coupled with constant changes of governments, have had an adverse effect on the promotion of a common goal. In addition, there are still concerns about coming out into the open instead of hiding away. We scientists do not need a lot: just peace to get on with our work in a secure environment."

Tamara replayed all that she had heard, in her head. To this day, everything that happened in the country in the immediate aftermath of the collapse of the Soviet Union continues to shed a negative light. The citizens of this small independent republic had endured much hardship, dumped at their doors. What had been the true impact of political and geopolitical events on the current foundations of their country?

The imbalance created by worthless politicians had had a devastating effect on the progress of Science.

Tamara now began to fully appreciate the reason why her professor had decided to wall himself up below ground, to continue his academic work. She also knew that there were many people who were in the position to support such work – enthusiasts and patrons who had the resources to reinstate all of Kyrgyzstan's scientists and release them from their current fate of having to work hidden away in near derelict buildings. However, all of them - politicians, academics, businessmen- were far too intent on their own survival, adjusting to the new regime as best as they could.

For twenty years, there had been no visible signs of any scientific development in the country. The day when Kyrgyzstan under its first enlightened president, would become a leader in Scientific fields, was still some way off. For now, with independence still in its infancy, the long suspension of development in any field- agriculture, science, industry, commerce or tourism-could not be overturned until the country was able to establish a more stable infrastructure and encourage investment from other countries.

Today, following the changes imposed by the first two distinctive regimes and a long battle for democracy, a new and more democratic regime is in place. It is to be hoped that Kyrgyzstan will now reap the fruits of its labours.

* * *

The Kyrgyz Socialist Republic was amongst the most powerful and developed countries of the fifteen republics of the USSR. Kirghizia (as the country was previously known) is geographically a mountainous country with an abundance of livestock and a rich tradition of agricultural industries. Natural resources also gave rise to the development of other land-related industries including the harnessing of natural hydroelectric power via the Toktogul dams, which boosted both industrial production and land irrigation.

The last First Secretary of the Republic in the Soviet era was Usubaliev. During his term of office, the personnel of the Republic were carefully selected to best endorse this leader's ideology. Several generations of government employees had been raised in the spirit of patriotism and it was a very purposeful period.

When Mikhail Gorbachev came to power, shattering changes took place in the higher echelons of government.

The structure of rule began to crumble and impacted on all fields, one way or another, across all fifteen republics. The effect amplified the destructive nature of areas within the socialist system that had reigned for over seventy years. In particular, it had a negative impact on human resources that were under direct instructions from Moscow. Corruption soared. The selfishness and recklessness of many civil servants led to complete devastation.

Under pressure, Gorbachev appointed a second deputy known as Comrade L to tackle corruption. With him, came further changes to the administration of the higher echelons. His experimental approach, which dispelled all previous principles, resulted in many irreversible errors of judgment on behalf of civil servants and the Union itself. Their devastating impact was felt throughout Kyrgyzstan and the other Soviet Republics of Central Asia

With the employment of poorly assigned personnel, industries were pushed to the brink of collapse.

When Kyrgyzstan first gained independence, industries experienced a period of total inertia.

Under the first President, there occurred further changes in personnel which later caused ruin across all sectors. Plants and factories were closed and looting became widespread. In agriculture many unemployed residents took over the fields, empty villages and farms, and began the cultivation of sugar beet. Land which had once been professionally farmed was cultivated by helpless citizens, resulting in chaos throughout the country for over fifteen years.

On one occasion, a senior official who was travelling south, stopped his car and began shouting at a group of locals who were busily tying up mulberry trees. "You fools! What are you doing to these trees?"

One of them replied "These are mulberry trees. Their young branches need to be bound like this so that later on, silkworm larvae will come to feed on the fresh leaves. The larvae will then produce natural silk." Humiliated, the official then started yelling at his driver for not telling him anything about this custom.

The traditional cultivation of larvae and silk processing have been practiced in these parts for thousands of years but the wave of ignorance illustrated by this incident was new and a sad reflection of what was happening during this whole critical period.

Many democrats and journalists who advocated 'freedom of speech' were imprisoned but eventually, the people of Kyrgyzstan revolted. After the first revolution, which addressed the struggle for a more independent and democratic system, people expected immediate change. Unfortunately, no such miracle appeared.

During the rule of the second President, things got worse and his period in office, which caused irreversible damage, proved the most brutal in the history of Kyrgyzstan. The elderly still refer to this period as 'an apocalypse'.

The country lived through uneasy times. The outflow of young people to Russia increased dramatically and many citizens were forced to migrate in order to find work to support their families.

During the second revolution, many young citizens of Kyrgyzstan were killed in a square in the centre of Bishkek. They had fought for democracy, freedom of speech and human rights. Now, commemorative rallies are held every year on 7th April and a monument has been erected as a constant reminder of the history and the tragic events that led to the formation of democracy.

It stands in eternal memory to these heroes.

* * *

Chapter 23

Underground Laboratory, Bishkek, July 2014

Tamara had one request of the professor: She wanted to inform Alexei of her good news. Professor Komarov made no objection.

As she said her farewells, she had to pinch herself to make sure that she had not dreamt it all.

For many years, she had been tormented by the fact that they had never concluded their research and now wondered whether the theme of her own research might be of some value. Perhaps she could help her former supervisor? The country had experienced turbulent times during its twenty years of independence, drastically altering the Kyrgyz people's outlook on life, but she could now see that things were gradually being pieced together, like tiles on a mosaic. Tamara was convinced that in this enlightened era, her knowledge should be used for the benefit of something higher; for the sake of Science itself.

The discovery of the secret laboratory would provide her with new opportunities to put into practice, her dedication to Science and bring powerful motivation and purpose to her life.

A strange letter was waiting for her when she returned home. It was unsigned and there was no sender's address. It simply stated "Don't worry, everything is under control."

She felt shaken by the letter and had no idea what it referred to. What was 'under control' and who was the author of this letter?

Breathing deeply to calm her nerves, Tamara sat down at her computer and tried to skype her daughter Ayganysh, who was in Scotland. No one was online. Tamara then sent an SMS on her mobile phone. There was an immediate response: Ayganysh and her husband were in a taxi, heading for Edinburgh airport. They were on their way home to Munich. Tamara felt a warm glow wash over her body.

Tamara went outside and hugged the maple tree at the bottom of her garden. Then suddenly, unable to contain her emotions any longer, she began to sob; releasing all of the anxiety and feelings of helplessness which she had had to endure.

She wept bitterly for all of the difficulties, fuelled by changing ideologies, that had plagued the lives of her people and especially, her former professor and co-workers, who had been forced to live like 'cold shadows'. When her tears were spent, Tamara felt calmer and her mind turned to Sinatra; allowing his soulful song about an invisible lover caress her inner ear.

A sudden thought then struck Tamara and in a state of high excitement, she ran into her house.

Opening the fridge, she pulled out some cheese and rye bread and then poured herself a shot of brandy.

She drank it in one draught, ate the bread and cheese, and automatically poured a second shot. Tamara then turned to the picture hanging in her kitchen, shook her head and downed her drink. She narrowed her eyes as she examined the picture more carefully, and then turning on her computer, began to write to her former colleague. In her email, she told Alexei all about the secret laboratory that now functioned from a city centre basement, and related the professor's extraordinary story. She asked whether Alexei would be interested in becoming involved in this secret project and if he could come to Bishkek for at least a few days.

Could they gather up their former team of scientists including Alexei, to re-engage in the project begun so long ago? She had always hoped for a sharp turn of events and now truly believed it possible. She wrote quickly and automatically, as if guided by an external force, firing proposals to all of the characters involved.

After a while, and with growing concern, she tried to call Ayganysh, but her attempts were again unsuccessful.

What was going on? It pained her that she could not reach her daughter but she felt more uneasy about the content of that anonymous letter. What could it mean? Was it somehow connected with her past?

Tamara reread the letter and even smelled the envelope.

She knew that her anxiety would keep her awake and so walked into the kitchen and drank another glass of brandy. Shortly after midnight, she was relieved to finally receive a call from her daughter. She sounded very tired and told Tamara that she would call again the next day to tell her everything that she had been doing.

Tamara didn't push her, but was concerned by how worried she sounded and wondered whether she was having problems with either her friends or Stefan.

It was now daybreak and Tamara, overcome by fatigue from the day's unexpected and remarkable events, crawled fully clothed into bed and immediately fell into a deep sleep.

The next day she received an email from Alexei.

"Hello dear Tamara. You can't imagine how happy I would be, to see you again. I will arrive on the first flight. I cannot begin to explain how I feel. It's like something has awoken inside me. I don't know why I've waited all these years to return to you! As for the news of our former boss and the laboratory hidden in the basement, my head is spinning! I can barely hope that it will soon be possible for us all to be reunited in our work! Please pick me up at the airport, but don't tell the professor I'm coming: I want it to be a big surprise.

Yours, Alexei"

* * *

Chapter 24

Meanwhile, in Munich…

The large house in the centre of the city, where Ayganysh and Stefan lived with their friend, had been completely turned over. A vase that had contained fresh flowers lay smashed on the floor and in each room, furniture had been toppled and scattered.

Schultz was standing next to the fridge in the small kitchen, nervously smoking a cigarette as he rummaged for ice. He wrapped a handful in a clean beige cloth and then held the bag of ice against the wound on his arm. Somewhere, hidden away, wafted the sound of women moaning. With the agility of a professional burglar, Schultz smashed the lock of the pantry door to check on the hostages and ignoring their pleas, closed the door and returned to the kitchen.

The two blindfolded hostages, who had inadvertently been caught up in this mess, were Ayganysh's friend Aisuluu, and Mrs Kate. They had been tied up and pushed into the cupboard by Schultz and his boss. Schultz had been given the house address by his contacts and had arrived by taxi that morning, expecting to find Stefan and Ayganysh.

When he knocked on the door, Mrs Kate had called out : "Who's there?"

He had pleasantly replied "Excuse me for bothering you but I'm lost and wonder if you could help me with directions?"

Mrs Kate was surprised to hear someone at her door since everyone living in the house had keys and it was unusual to receive callers at such an early hour. Nevertheless, and suspecting nothing untoward, she opened the door to a handsome stranger.

She and Aisuluu had just spring-cleaned the house: a newly laundered cloth covered the table and the air was filled with the scent of fresh flowers. Upstairs, someone was singing in the bathroom.

The landlady quickly grew annoyed by her visitor's awkward and insensitive manners. He had unfolded a large map and apparently expected to be invited into her home. He even asked for a glass of water. However, his charm soon won her over and unable to see the map clearly she asked him into the hall. She fetched him a drink and timidly explained that she was expecting family and was in the middle of preparations for their arrival. He didn't touch the water and Mrs Kate felt a growing unease. The dark expression on his face was no longer that of a gentleman who was simply seeking directions, and his physical presence seemed to bear down on her. Suddenly, Schultz made a grab for her and with great force, pushed her into the lounge and onto the sofa.

Mrs Kate let out a loud cry as she tried to push him away. She desperately tried to reach for the phone that lay on the coffee table. Her efforts were intercepted by Schultz and in the ensuing struggle; they fell against the table, upsetting the vase of flowers.

"Aargh! Help! Aisuluu!"

Shultz then straddled her and grasped her by the throat but even though her cry for help was barely a whisper, it alerted Aisuluu who immediately raced down from the bathroom, screaming.

Unable to pull Schultz's hands from Mrs Kate's neck, Aisuluu bit him hard on the wrist. In retaliation, Schultz threw her across the room but without losing any time, she picked up a stool and flung it against her attacker's back. He cried out in pain and releasing his grip on Mrs Kate, staggered to the floor coughing and breathless.

Schultz quickly recovered and leaping to his feet, made a lunge for Aisuluu, grabbing her wet hair.

For a split second, as he held Aisuluu fast, Schultz was reminded of his wife, Lauren and he trembled as he inhaled the scent of the balm on her damp hair and gazed upon her beautiful, youthful body which still wet, was barely covered by her bathrobe. She had a similar feisty spirit and he was momentarily taken back to the exact moment when he had saved Lauren from the hunters.

Caught in this daydream, he released his grip on Aisuluu and seizing the opportunity, she made for her phone and terrified, started dialling the police. However, there was no escaping Schultz, and in an instant, the phone was knocked from her hand.

She could do no more and standing in front of him and high on adrenaline she repeated over and over: "Please, take whatever you want! What do you want from us? Who are you?"

Schultz made no response. Instead of the figure of an unknown young woman, his mind's eye saw only Lauren. She needed his help. He had to save her! As he moved forward to comfort her, the spell was broken by further pleading from his captive "I have nothing to offer you! What do you want from us? I have no money. Take everything that you can carry, but don't kill us ... Please! I have a baby at home! My parents are old. They have no one else to take care of them and without me they will simply starve! Please ..."

Aisuluu did not understand why this man did not appear to hear anything she said nor acknowledge her desperation.

She was therefore taken by complete surprise when gazing at her tenderly, he stepped forward and wrapped her in a blanket and soothingly, told her:

"Don't worry, I'll save you, Lauren ... I'm here now... "

Suddenly the front door opened and they could all hear the hoarse voice of a taxi driver exclaim "Whoa, Schultz!"

He then marched up the hall and into the lounge and seizing Schultz by the shoulder, slapped him hard across the face.

"Are you crazy? Are you determined to fail this operation? This young girl is not Lauren! Lauren has long gone! Wake up, you donkey!" The taxi driver raised his hand for a second strike but this time, Schultz was ready and rose to defend himself by head-butting his attacker.

It was a violent blow, which threw the man to the ground, but he immediately sat up and nursing his broken nose, yelled "Don't you dare mess up this the operation, you idiot"

He then pulled out his revolver and pointed it directly at Schultz.

Aisuluu and Mrs Kate watched the scene in terror, clutching each other and hardly daring to breathe, from the far corner of the room.

"Excuse me boss" With a shake of his head, Shultz seemed to have awoken from a state of unconsciousness.

"Hey you: Young lady! What's your name? Come and help me!" the taxi driver crudely beckoned towards Aisuluu who was huddled in fear, trying to look invisible.

"Leave her alone and go and wash your face" interjected Schultz, still a little bewitched by the girl who reminded him so much of his wife.

The taxi driver quickly splashed water from the kitchen tap over his bleeding face and re-emerged, holding his broken nose.

"Lock them both in the closet, we need them as hostages. Moreover, do nothing else until the two we are looking for turn up. That's an order!"

Aisuluu and Mrs Kate were blindfolded and locked in the cupboard and to ensure that Schultz did not hamper the plan, the taxi driver slipped the key into his pocket. They all then settled down to wait.

Soon afterwards, the taxi driver received a message on his mobile phone. Stefan and Ayganysh would shortly be arriving at the airport in Munich. They had not boarded the ferry.

"Well, it looks like we've netted our fish." He announced smugly, still staring at the ceiling to stem the blood flowing from his nose.

"We should now be able to hook the attention of that bold scoundrel who stole those documents and ruined my operation." With a satisfied smile, the taxi driver went out and slamming the door behind him, raced to the airport to intercept Ayganysh and Stefan.

* * *

The man posing as the taxi driver had headed up the original mission and was still Schultz's boss. This secret organization played a double game and had framed and destroyed many experienced agents. They were still looking for Lauren and her accomplice.

Half of the money in the briefcase, which Schultz had commandeered after he had murdered the scientist's wife, comprised bonds, which could not be used abroad. Schultz was so angered by this discovery, that he stuck them on the walls of a toilet in a Hungarian coffee shop. They encapsulated the total collapse of the USSR and the end of the Cold War,

The owner of the cafe was so thankful for this special gift, that he offered him a room for the night. Schultz was waiting for further instructions but things changed unexpectedly. The explosion and the subsequent fire destroyed all that remained of their mission and the operation failed.

* * *

Chapter 25

Stefan and Ayganysh arrive home

The large concourse of Munich airport's main terminal was teeming with tourists. Many were enjoying the hospitality of the fine, Bavarian - style restaurants and stared in awe at their surroundings. The building, constructed from glass and steel, was a prime example of modernist architecture and employed cutting edge, German technology.

Stefan and Ayganysh tried to phone Aisuluu and Mrs Kate but could not reach them. They finished their coffee and joined the taxi queue. To their surprise, a taxi driver with a bandaged nose and strange accent immediately approached them. They gladly accepted his courteous services but were surprised when he did not ask for their address. As he headed for the city centre, it seemed that he already knew where they lived.

"Wait, you don't know our address and we want to stop off at the police station on the way, if you don't mind." Stefan demanded as firmly as he could.

"Oh, excuse me, of course." replied the taxi driver; but then, to their horror, he pulled on a mask and flicked a switch to lock the passenger doors and windows.

Grey gas began to infiltrate the cab and within seconds, Stefan and Ayganysh, were slumped unconscious, on the back seat.

* * *

Still groggy, they found themselves bound to chairs in front of the two hostage takers, in the hall of an apartment that looked familiar. As they watched the two men pacing up and down, they grew increasingly worried about their future.

Who were these men? What did they want? Why had they taken them hostage?

There was clearly some conflict between them and voices were raised as they argued long and hard, at the other end of the room. The taxi driver with the bandaged nose who had collected them from the airport was glaring angrily at the second man. As he watched them, Stefan suddenly realised that he recognised this character. It was the man he had encountered outside his tent on their last night at Notrom Castle.

He felt as though he had been plunged into some sort of hell and fighting the nausea and headache sustained by the poisonous gas, he tried to piece together his memories of that night.

However, the effects of the gas were still strong: the room spun and when he looked at the ceiling, he saw double and then triple images of the chandelier.

Stefan desperately needed to figure out how and under what circumstances, he and his wife had become involved in this situation and so switched his attention to what the men were discussing.

"Ha! I have him at last! There will be no chance of him escaping me this time!" The taxi driver laughed as he poured himself a large brandy, drank it in one shot, and lit a cigarette.

Stefan felt as if he were underwater: images swam in front of his eyes and the men's voices washed over him like dull echoes from the deep. The world continued to spin illusively around him. He screwed up his eyes tightly, trying to correct his vision and looked towards his wife Ayganysh, who was sitting next to him. Her mouth was also sealed but she tried to send him some sort of signal with her eyes. He blinked back, in an attempted warning for her to sit still and avoid drawing attention to herself.

Meanwhile, Stefan surreptitiously tried to free himself from the ropes that bound him so that he could somehow help Ayganysh.

These were clearly no ordinary thieves but what were they were after?

Stefan took a deep breath and realized that he and his wife were completely alone and helpless. What should they do? It dawned on him that they could be using Ayganysh as bait to attract the attention of someone else. Who was her father? He again honed in on previous conversations about him but found no further clues to his identity. The men repeatedly spoke of Lauren and her alleged partner in crime.

Stefan felt exhausted by his attempts to understand what linked them to this other, unknown, situation.

Schultz looked at Ayganysh and then sharply splashed her face with cold water to speed up her recovery.

The men were clearly short of time and worried about something.

"Come on: get up" Schultz sounded awkward as he spoke to Ayganysh. His boss meanwhile, continued to sit on the couch drinking and smoking, with a nasty sneer on his face.

Schultz then pulled her chair forwards and untying her ropes, gently guided Ayganysh by her elbow towards the window.

Frightened by what might happen next, Stefan became highly agitated and began to whine loudly. Schultz immediately swung around and kicked him hard in the face, causing Stefan's chair to crash to the floor. The young man was instantly stunned by the blow but very quickly, resumed his struggle to break free and rescue his wife.

At that moment, Schultz's mobile phone rang. He looked at the caller's number in surprise before answering:

"Hello, yes Schultz speaking." He then hesitated as if confused, and breathing heavily continued:

"Lauren?! ... Is that you? ... What? Where? On the next street?" He repeated the caller's every word.

"Schultz! Don't move!" His boss leapt from the couch as if intent on throwing him from the window. Schultz however was only thinking of Lauren and paid no heed to him. Grabbing Ayganysh he rushed to the window to see whether his wife was really waiting for him outside.

Then Shultz suddenly collapsed to the floor as if poleaxed.

Now free, Ayganysh immediately crawled to Stefan and automatically began to untie him.

When she looked back at her captor, she closed her eyes and let out a silent scream. Schultz lay dead on the floor in an ever increasing pool of blood, with eyes wide open and a bullet hole in the front of his head.

She barely had time to register the horror of it all, when positioned on the roof of the adjacent building; the sniper took aim at the taxi driver who was standing aghast by the couch. The shot, which flew through the open window, caught the man on the shoulder, sending his own weapon into the air.

"No one will touch my daughter; let alone hold her hostage. I have been looking to revenge you scum for a long time!" The sniper surveyed the scene from his hiding place and lifting his transmitter, coldly gave orders for the wounded man to be picked up. His aim had been deliberate: he wanted this one alive.

There quickly followed a loud hammering on the door and armed soldiers burst in and immediately surrounded the wounded taxi driver. Military personnel then helped Ayganysh to untie Stefan and without a word of explanation, dragged Schultz's body and his boss out of the apartment. The man disguised as the taxi driver was a dangerous criminal wanted by secret organizations and had been hunted for many years. He had finally been caught.

Stefan hugged Ayganysh tight and then covered his face with his hands and sobbed uncontrollably.

More military police arrived shortly afterwards and hearing groans and banging from the cupboard at the far end of the corridor, released Aisuluu and Mrs. Kate. Once they had checked that none of the hostages were injured, the questioning began.

After the police had left, they continued to sit for a long time, staring at each other in silence but eventually, someone got up to turn on the lights and one by one, they began to busy themselves by cleaning up the mess.

Mrs Kate and Aisuluu prepared supper whilst Stefan and Ayganysh laid the table: each of them drawing comfort from performing routine tasks after the day's trauma.

No one uttered a single word, as if everything was happening in a silent film, until exchanging glances between each other, Stefan and Ayganysh decided to tell their friends about their trip to Notrom Castle and the amazing people they had met in Scotland.

Suddenly, everyone came to life, as if awoken from a long sleep. They eagerly poured over the photographs of historical monuments and the rugged Scottish landscape, and then listened in awe as Stefan related how he had saved a crazy old man from drowning himself in a shallow pond.

The next day, Stefan's grandfather called to say that he was on his way home, driving the car that he had collected from the ferry at Zeebrugge. Stefan and Ayganysh had told him nothing about their escapades and had asked their friends to do likewise so as not to worry the old man. He was therefore left under the misunderstanding that they had chosen to reject his gift of the car.

Arriving back at the family home in Leipzig, he parked the car and then curiosity got the better of him. He slowly opened up the back of the old car to reveal the secret compartment containing the radiotelephone device. The red light on the top of the message machine was flashing just like in the old days. Even though he had retired long ago, his fingers automatically tapped in a code and the machine immediately responded. Erich started to smile as the machine advised him he had one message. He'd assumed that he would never again hear anything from the machine. The message was short and from one of his former colleagues – Lauren.

"Dear Erich. Our mission is finally complete. We got both of them. One of them has been dispatched but the other is alive. We need to meet to discuss some little issues. Please respond. Over."

Chapter 26

Stefan's Grandfather

Later that day, Ayganysh received a letter with the following instructions:

Come to the church in the city centre at 3pm tomorrow. Sit in the third row and look behind you. You will see a boy, a little younger than you. He is your half-brother; the son I had with my wife Lauren. Please do not tell Tamara anything about the events of the past few days. It would only distress her and everything is now under control.

Your father.

P.S. Burn this letter and flush the ashes down the sink. It must not be traced.

Ayganysh wept for a long time. She began to understand the significant role that her father played in her life. He was there to protect her and it must have been he who anonymously and without fail, sent her mother fresh roses on every holiday.

She remembered fondly, how Tamara often told her friends about her dizzying short romance. Love can survive any threat of destruction to humanity and makes life appear less cruel and grim! There is love in us all: a special kind of magic that lives in our hearts.

The next day Ayganysh was elusive about her reasons for going into town. She boarded a bus and made sure that she reached the church at exactly three o'clock.

Meanwhile, Stefan phoned his grandfather to apologise for daring to leave his car on the ferry unattended. He promised to visit him at the weekend and help him weed the garden. Stefan felt tremendous remorse about abandoning his grandfather's precious gift on the ferry but knew that he could never explain the exceptional circumstances that had forced him to do so. He knew that his grandfather would be upset, and this saddened him more.

True to form, his grandfather in turn cursed the youth of today's slavish devotion to high technology that to his mind, was a complete waste of time. Why couldn't they recognise the quality of traditional mechanics?

After the conversation on the phone with Stefan, his grandfather stared out of the window for a moment then picked up his daily newspaper and went to the kitchen. As he sipped his tea, he found himself mulling things over.

"Maybe I need to own up to my grandson and by explaining my past, instil in him, the value of the car which I gave him?" Then with a chuckle, he mused: "Or maybe not!"

His thoughts then turned to Lauren; the beautiful woman who had asked him to be part of Operation Budapest. He had been consigned to drive some man away from a building. Little did he know that the building was going to be blown to bits, sending shock waves through him and his passenger...

"How interesting: I wonder whatever happened to that poor British spy? I can still remember his name. Fred Rodgers!" He often thought about those days and all the intrigues and tensions of that Cold War period.

He hoped that should he ever confide in his grandson, Stefan would understand and never pass judgement on his grandfather's past.

This car had been a present from Lauren to commemorate the end of the Cold War, when East and West Germany finally became one country.

* * *

In the middle of Munich stands the Frauenkirche. This is one of the country's most famous churches. Built in the fifteenth century to a 5th century design, it boasts twin towers, 99 metres high.

The renowned acoustics create a magical atmosphere and the visitors who flock to the daily organ recitals feel themselves transposed as they allow the music to wash over them.

As instructed, Ayganysh found the third row and sat down quietly. She looked behind her.

The young man who was sitting in the next pew smiled and she returned his smile. He then quietly held out a book and nodded as a sign that she should take it.

Aware of his background, Ayganysh could not resist studying his face for features similar to her own.

He had a firm physique and upright posture and his skin and hair were fair. His smallish brown eyes gave him a confident and slightly aloof air.

Ayganysh turned and took the book and when she opened the marked page, saw a picture of her father and the young man together.

She stared at the photograph for a long time and tears rolled down her cheeks. Tamara had no pictures but now Ayganysh was finally able to see what her father looked like. Studying it carefully, she realised that it solved a mystery that had tormented her all her life.

On the reverse of the picture were the date and the name of the place where the photograph had been taken.

Ayganysh put the book in her handbag and dabbed at her tears with a handkerchief. She immediately wanted to look at it again but turned instead to admire to her brother. But the young man was no longer there. In a matter of seconds, he had simply disappeared.

"Oh God: thank you for these moments of bliss. The anguish that has been brewing within me throughout my life has finally gone: What better place to discover my father than this special church filled with ethereal music?!" As Ayganysh made to leave the church, she noticed a woman sitting in the far corner watching her. She smiled sweetly and gave Ayganysh a little nod, before hastily walking out of the church.

"Who was she?" wondered Ayganysh "Lauren?"

This mysterious woman had a delicate beauty and a passion for life which shone from her penetrating grey eyes. She could have been anyone, but there was something about her fair skin and strong features that resembled Ayganysh's half- brother. The girl was more than convinced that the woman was indeed Lauren.

Ayganysh took a long walk across the city. Overwhelmed by a flood of emotions, she experienced a sense of being re-born. She had been upset and confused by her father's strict instructions to tell no one about his letter and it broke her heart not to tell her mum, but now she and her father were bonded by their own secret!

Bolot finished his organ recital and smiled happily. He had not felt so inspired for a very long time. He thanked the minister, handed over the keys and wishing him goodnight, stepped outside. The evening promised dizzying memories.

Bolot patted his moustache and lit up a Chesterfield cigarette. He lingered contentedly for a while, watching passers-by, and then walked quickly towards a dark car. He climbed in and turning to the driver, gave her a satisfied 'thumbs up' sign:

"Everything is under control. Let's go, Lauren."

He quietly wiped his tears and then hugged her close and kissed her. Both of them looked from side to side and then sped through the streets of Munich to an unknown destination.

Chapter 27

Manas Airport, Bishkek 2014

It was early morning. The tops of the mountains were still covered with snow despite it being July. Tamara had lived in Bishkek for many years yet this morning, felt as though she were noticing its beauty for the first time. The grass around the airport shone vibrant green as the gentle summer sun broke through the mist that enveloped the airport. Tamara had been unable to sleep since the arrival of Alexei's message the previous day. It had announced that he would be arriving today and now, as she waited to meet him, she kept her nerves at bay by quietly singing.

The events of recent days, which had descended like a whirlwind, were almost overwhelming and the good news about Komarov had momentarily overshadowed any concerns about Alexei.

Many years had passed, and she and Alexei were still living alone and apart: she was here in Bishkek and he was on the other side of the border. She felt unsure of herself and did not know what to expect of Alexei. After all, he had never made any explicit declaration of his feelings for her, although there had been hints...

The image of the painting in her kitchen and the girl's invisible lover were always with her. Could it be that the scene related to her innermost feelings for Alexei? Was he 'the one'?

"Bother! Something doesn't quite fit." she said quietly to herself, trying not to attract the attention of a waitress who just brought her a second cup of coffee.

She shook her head, smiling sweetly. The view from the window was magnificent with the sun shining on the distant snow-capped mountains. It was still hot and Tamara wished it would rain a little, to cool things down.

She then sat back to enjoy the hustle and bustle of passengers flowing through the airport: everyday life where people converged and then dispersed.

* * *

Chapter 28

Alexei

Meanwhile, Alexei was sitting on the plane, also feeling nervous. Thoughts about Tamara had haunted him for many years. The flight attendant brought him a whisky on the rocks and as he sipped his drink, he flicked through some old black and white photographs. From time to time, he smiled and then shook his head, sighing deeply.

He then put on his headphones and let classical music wash over him as he allowed his mind to wander back in time.

He saw himself emerging from the subway near the ZUM in Frunze and hearing the sparkling laughter of several girls.

As he turned, he saw her: A still very young Tamara with a group of friends. They stepped onto the street and were instantly swept away by the crowd.

The Academic Council had just hired Alexei as a scientific research assistant and he was now a member of the commission established by Professor Komarov to recruit young professionals. He had an important day ahead and looking at his watch, knew that he had to hurry.

Suddenly someone tapped him on the back and he turned to see an old gypsy woman who had been reading fortunes in the subway. She smiled at Alexei and asked if he could spare a couple of minutes to help her. He took her hand and guided her out of the subway, thinking that the morning had started rather strangely.

Alexei jumped on a bus and made it to the lab on time. He was pleased that he was able to work uninterrupted for the rest of the day.

Something however was gnawing at his heart. At the end of the day, he was on his way out when Komarov appeared in his office. The professor had come to tell him about a couple of students who were expected to arrive the next day. One of them, named Tamara, came strongly recommended by her supervisor with whom she had worked closely. She had recently moved from Leningrad for family reasons.

"Okay, I'll make sure I'm in early." replied Alexei, closing up his office.

That night, he could not get to sleep. The internal gnawing grew into a vivid memory of the charming girl he'd seen laughing at the subway. His mind would not give him peace. He went out to his balcony and smoked a few cigarettes. He had always been sceptical about gypsies' fortune- telling powers but feeling desperate, found himself being swayed by a particular notion:

"Tomorrow I'll find that gypsy woman! Perhaps she can tell me something about that girl?"

After soothing his racing mind with a plan of action, exhaustion kicked in and he fell into a sound sleep. The next morning he failed to hear his alarm and when he finally woke with a start, he instantly realised he had slept in. Knowing that he was meant to be early, he duly panicked and was still pulling on his clothes as he hailed a taxi in the street outside his apartment. He was five minutes late for the morning meeting and all of the new students were already gathered in the large office. He tumbled through the door and was immediately arrested by the sight of a familiar, charming smile.

Alexei stood in a stupor but was then spotted by Komarov who beckoned him forward so that he could be introduced to the group.

The audience started whispering and some of them even began to laugh softly. Alexei felt uncomfortable. What was wrong? Did he look weird? Why were they all smiling as if they felt sorry for him?

Alexei familiarised the students with the main tasks of the project and the special laboratory where, if successful in their interviews, they would be working under Komarov. He then asked them to provide their contact details and fill in a form, prior to being interviewed.

At the end of the session, Tamara approached him, smiling brightly. She introduced herself and then in a quiet whisper, told Alexei that his socks did not match!

Alexei who prided himself on his exquisite dress sense was at first dumbfounded but then seeing the funny side, grinned at Tamara and they both burst out laughing.

"Sorry! I overslept this morning."

He was so happy to see her again that he could not care less about his different coloured socks and it would not have mattered if even his shoes had not matched.

He only had eyes for the charming girl whom he had first seen at the subway the day before and could not believe that here they were, sharing a joke together!

From then on, Alexei and Tamara became close friends. Because she had been selected to join Komarov's handpicked team, they found themselves working in the same lab.

Each morning they greeted each other warmly and then focused on their individual assignments, which were submitted directly to Komarov's office.

One weekend, whilst walking in the park, Alexei noticed the fortune-teller. She immediately approached him and smiling, quietly took his hand.

"Your destiny is in your hands, young man! Do not miss your chance!"

Before he could ask her more, she was gone.

Now sitting on the plane, Alexei reflected again, on what she had told him:

"Your destiny is in your hands" - a fortune teller told me,
She blinked at me, and then disappeared.
Without any understanding of what she meant
I have wandered through life
And the years spent without you
Dull days and nights, without season or dawns
Passed in a blank haze.
My destiny is in my hands
I just needed to believe that
The lines in my palms were guiding me to you
I strayed from destiny's path, a hundred times
But felt like a ghost amongst even my friends
The day that I first saw your sweet smile
Felt like the storm clouds, holding my dreams
Had finally burst open,
Pouring eternal joy into my life.

Feeling nervous and excited about seeing Tamara, he ordered another whisky and resumed his daydream. He dearly wished that his dreams would come true. All he wanted was for them to be together and for him to make her happy.

A flute-player played a tango for us,
And we danced all night long in that secluded place
The rain drummed down in tandem with the beat
And the ripples of the raindrops in the puddles
Echoed the sensuous bend of your hips
And the curve of your passionate lips
As they whispered words of love and magic
Our wet bodies gently came together
And our hearts beat in unison
At one with the music
We spent the summer like Turgenev's heroes,
Among the poplars and birch groves.
Love you, love you not
A daisy sang, counting its petals
As they blew away in the gentle breeze
Like angels' wings.

* * *

Alexei glanced at his watch and realising that they would soon be landing, went to the small lavatory to freshen up.

In the airport, Tamara heard the announcement that the Istanbul to to Bishkek flight had landed and her heartbeat quickened.

As she watched the first passengers appearing, Tamara struggled to calm her breathing. What was happening to her? What was the cause of this tide of confusing emotions: The awakening of long dormant passion? Or guilt? She had not experienced such intense feelings for a very long time.

Then suddenly, she saw him. Her Alexei! He was still the handsome man she remembered, with his elegant posture and piercing eyes. Apart from a slight greying around his temples, he had changed little during his years of living abroad.

She felt the ground shift slightly below her feet then oblivious to anything around her, ran to meet him. They hugged each other tightly and kissed. It was their first passionate kiss.

"Well, welcome Alexei!" It was Tamara who spoke first.

"It has been far too long, Tamara! Hello!" Alexei kept a tight grip on her arms as if afraid that she would run off.

He stared at her fondly and immediately fell to his knees. Then plucking up courage, he produced a beautiful antique ring and looking intensely into her eyes, asked:

"Tamara, will you marry me?"

"Do you remember those years, long ago and our trip to Lake Issyk-Kul? I desperately wanted to spend the evenings with you or run away with you to the lake. I spent two days in a row, waiting at your door to give you flowers that I'd plucked from the fields. You did not appear. I should have been more determined!"

"But Alexei; that was such a long time ago! I was very young." She silenced his lips with her index finger and tenderly kissed him.

Feeling as though she had been transported to some magical, fairy tale paradise, she burst into tears as she gave him the answer he had been waiting for.

"I will!"

Onlookers, who had witnessed this scene, burst into a round of applause but Tamara and Alexei, now caught in a passionate embrace did not hear or see any of this.

They emerged from the airport under a spectacular sunrise and exited in a taxi towards their new life together.

* * *

Chapter 29

Foggy Hill, Scotland, June 2015

"Kaa – lin! Kakalin – kakalinka moya!" Cecile tried to repeat the chorus, playing the old tape over and over again: She had been trying to learn the song for many months. Cecile had long been in contact with a gentleman from a Russian dating site for single pensioners. She had shared her secret with only a few of her close friends but the whole town seemed to know about it and she suspected that some of the older villagers were jealous of her romantic mood. There was no harm in it and yet some of the rumours aimed to upset her.

After Rodgers had been buried by the villagers, a strange languor fell upon Foggy Hill. People found their daily lives monotonous and everything felt as dull and tedious as the weather itself.

Cecile was pleased to find tenants who promised to look after her small garden, so she felt happier about her trip to visit her new beau. He wrote letters every day and promised to show her the whole of Russia by train. As she re-read his most recent letter, she was glad that her new beau wanted to share everything that was happening in Moscow, where he lived in a chalet.

"Dear Cecile. I cannot wait for your arrival. My son recently got a promotion at work. He is now Colonel Zverev! I am very happy for him. I am sure he deserved it. Yes, I will teach you how to cook borsch. This is a traditional Russian dish."

Cecile opened up a book of Russian recipes she had recently purchased and started looking for a photo of the famous Russian borsch. As she surveyed the picture, she thought it looked promising.

She had recently had a fight with a local 'Don Juan.' He clearly opposed Cecile's political views and in the local hostelry had accused her of being 'a wee red-faced Tory!'

Cecile had actively supported the Conservative Party since her youth and when David Cameron extended his term as Prime Minister for another five years in order to complete the implementation of his policies and launch new, ambitious initiatives, she had opened a bottle of whisky in secret celebration. She was quietly proud of his patriotism and inexhaustible energy and believed that the British didn't know how lucky they were to have such a competent leader to navigate the country through the economic mess left by the previous Socialist Party.

The local 'Don Juan' had never stood a chance. He was duly summoned by the various Chairmen and Chairwomen of local clubs and societies and within a blink of an eye, found himself shown the door and his social life reduced to nil.

Cecile did not attach great importance to everything that happened in this small town and the rumours that went around. At her age, it was not worth the bother and after all, incredible adventures were waiting for her and her new Russian beau. She decided that life lived in hatred should be completely erased, on either side of the world!

Cecile had no reason to harbour hostile feelings. After all, time had passed and they had survived the war, with all its fear and hardships, and had rebuilt Britain.

Nevertheless, as she emptied her suitcase containing old, yellowed letters sent by her father during the First World War, she could barely hold back her bitter tears. She didn't need to read them; their lines were etched in her memory. She carefully set aside his photograph, taken from her bookcase, and packed it away with his letters. She also wrapped up her old gas mask, kept as a memento from another war; the 'cold war' of her youth.

Before leaving, she went to Rodgers' grave where she laid a small bunch of daisies.

"I'm sorry, Fred I know you wanted to share something with me but I was never able to find the time. I knew your wife as a little girl growing up in this town. I remember teaching her at school and listening to her Christmas concert piano recitals. They improved every year. You were lucky to find such a good wife. Your past always seemed very dark to me but we have long lived in peaceful times. Now I have new lease of life! Do not laugh at me when I tell you I am off to Moscow to learn how to cook borsch!" As she spoke, her face broke into a smile.

Her friend waved her off on the bus bound for Edinburgh Airport. She bought some coffee, looked up at the leaden clouds of Edinburgh and sighed with hidden happiness. She was embarking on something new. There would be many adventures ahead as she journeyed through Russia.

* * *

Chapter 30

Notrom Castle, Foggy Hill, Scotland. July 2015

The residents of the small town of Foggy Hill gave hearty applause to the performance of a talented young singer from Argentina. She and her family had come to Scotland a few years previously and within a short period, Esmeralda had been warmly accepted as a member of the local community. With a wonderful voice, which would one day ensure her a career as an opera singer, she had surprised and delighted the audience with her talent.

The concert, which also included recitals by many other musicians on that balmy day in July, uplifted everyone's spirits and left tourists and locals alike, with a sense of peace and hope for a harmonious future.

Thus, life in that unusual and somewhat enigmatic place continued its flow.

HERTFORDSHIRE PRESS

Title List